HAUNTED
LIVERPOOL 21

For Sky High Symphony

© Tom Slemen 2013

Published by The Bluecoat Press, Liverpool
Book design by www.march-design.co.uk
Printed by Melita Press, Malta

ISBN 9781908457141

All rights reserved. No part of this publication may be reproduced, stored in a retrieval system, or transmitted in any form or by any means, electronic, mechanical, photocopying, recording or otherwise, without prior permission from the publisher.

Tom Slemen

HAUNTED
LIVERPOOL 21

THE BLUECOAT PRESS

Contents

THE AINTREE VAMPIRE	6
HIGHWAY INVADERS	9
THE MIRROR GHOST	11
CLEARED BY A MEDIUM	14
SHORE LEAVE	20
THE WAVERTREE THING	23
LIVERPOOL'S LITTLE PEOPLE	25
DISAPPEARING DOHERTY	31
MING IN MY EAR	39
DAYDREAM NUMBER FIVE	42
TRUTH WINE	48
ASK MR ARIES	50
WALTON WITCHERY	54
A STRANGE WALTON HALL AVENUE HAUNTING	63
THE PURPLE SHADES	69
STRANGE ABDUCTIONS	73

CARNATES	82
BEYOND THESE PRISON WALLS	89
THE FACE	99
A TRAGIC HAUNTING	102
SOME HALLOWEEN TALES	107
THE MUGGER ON LARK LANE	117
THE SECRET OF CASTLE HILL	122
GLASGOW SMILE	124
THE LAD IN THE HALLWAY	127
FACULTY X	130
MR MEDUSA	135
HUMPTY WAS PUSHED	142
THE VAMPIRES OF HARTINGTON ROAD	147
THE ROMANCE OF INANIMATE OBJECTS	161
THE THING IN THE BEDKNOB	169

The Aintree Vampire

Around 3.40am on the Tuesday morning of 3 September 1963, Ron, a petty thief from Bootle, was trying to break into a lock-up in a certain alleyway behind Aintree's Greenwich Road. He tried picking the padlock on the big green wooden door but the picklock rods just wouldn't work their magic, possibly because the lock seemed rather rusted, and so Ron took out his trusty old jemmy, checking up and down the alley, just in case there was someone about. Not a soul stirred at this unearthly hour, and above the rooftops of Greenwich Road, a full moon shone down, but Ron was luckily in the shadows, shielded from its revealing silvery light.

He was just about to try and prise the padlock off the door with the short crowbar when he thought he heard a noise behind him and to his right. He turned slowly to the direction of the real or imagined sound and saw something he still cannot explain to this day. A tall (about six feet and four inches at least) slim figure of an elderly but distinguished-looking man in a long cape stood at the mouth of the entry, enveloped in a faint blue phosphorescence. His white hair stuck out in pointed tufts on either side of his head like little devil horns, and on his face was a straight, white, well-trimmed moustache and a snowy Vandyke beard. Beneath the dark swept-back eyebrows, was a pair of bulging eyes whose irises were bright compared to the dark eyeballs, and gave a piercing, mischievous stare.

Ron instinctively lifted the leather-gloved hand which held the jemmy, intending to strike out at the entity if it approached, when the mouth of the apparition opened slightly to reveal two rows of long pointed teeth. Ron turned on his heels and ran off down the alleyway to the sound of cackling laughter. A heavy smoker on the wrong side of thirty, Ron found himself out of breath as he bolted down Inglis Road. Forced to slow, he looked over his shoulder, and saw to his great relief that he was not being pursued by what had surely been a ghost of some sort.

In the ten years Ron had indulged in a life of crime, he had never seen anything remotely supernatural, but on reaching Longmoor Lane, there was the old man in the long flowing cape, coming towards him from the top of Poulter Road. The blue radiance still surrounded him, but it was less pronounced in the gleaming moonlight. Ron instinctively tightened his grasp on the handle of the crowbar in his inside jacket pocket, but knew it was useless. How on earth could he injure something that looked as if it was already dead?

He ran off, confused, and upon reaching the Prince George pub, he looked back again – and saw that the figure seemed to be gliding along towards him, its cloak billowing out with the forward movement. Ron cursed as he took flight down Greenwich Road – a road which ran alongside Kirkdale Cemetery – aware of the distant laughter. He turned again to see the vampiric creature round the corner where the Prince George stood and accelerate towards him. Ron increased his speed until he came upon a welcoming sight in the distance: two policemen coming his way on their beat up Greenwich Road. Quickly jettisoning his jemmy and leather gloves behind the cemetery wall, he hurried towards the policemen – the irony of which did not escape him. The constables eyed him suspiciously, but a panting Ron turned and pointed to the cloaked pursuer – who had now stopped dead about three hundred yards away. The policemen wanted to know Ron's full name and if he had ever been in trouble with the law before. Ron shook his head and said he had been returning from his cousin's party in Walton Vale and urged the constables to tackle the maniac. 'Look at him go!' one of the policemen remarked as the eerie figure suddenly ran off at an incredible speed. Within a few seconds he was lost to sight.

Ron became a reformed character soon after that encounter, and gave up his life of crime. He died a few years ago, and when I spoke to him in 2004, he was intrigued to discover that I had received many reports of the so-called Aintree Vampire over the years.

In 1971, a very nimble cloaked figure was seen running at a phenomenal speed through Kirkdale Cemetery by scores of children one autumn evening, and in the 1980s I received two reports of what was undoubtedly the same silver-haired bogeyman from off-duty nurses from a certain hospital who had been chased along Lower House Lane by the uncanny cloaked figure. I also mentioned the entity on a BBC radio programme one afternoon and was afterwards deluged with calls and emails about the 'vampire'. Many of the callers said the figure always went to ground at Kirkdale Cemetery whenever it was chased, and one woman had even seen the fanged phantasm as recently as 2010 in West Derby Cemetery.

Elaine, from West Derby, who was 53 when I interviewed her in 2006, was a beautiful young 20-year-old blonde in 1973 and lived just a stone's throw from Aintree's famous racecourse. One freezing February night of that year, Elaine's sleep was disturbed by the sensation of someone getting into bed with her. She opened her eyes to find a stranger's head resting on the pillow next to hers. It was too dark in the bedroom to make out the man's features, but he had a pointed light-coloured beard and moustache and white hair. His breath had a sweet smell reminiscent of lavender.

Just before Elaine screamed for help, the creepy bed-hopper whispered something unintelligible. Elaine threw herself out of bed and ran out of the room in hysterics. When her parents and older brother went into the girl's bedroom, there was no one there – but the bedroom window was wide open and the February gales were fiercely blowing the nets and curtains about. Elaine's father maintained that the 'ghost' had been nothing more than a product of a particularly realistic nightmare, but Elaine asked him how a figment of a dream could open her bedroom windows wide. There was no history of hauntings at Elaine's house, and I feel that the thing which got into her bed, possibly to seduce her, was the fanged white-haired entity known as the Aintree Vampire. I have tried to unravel the obscure history of the Aintree Vampire (or whatever he is) for some time now, but to date he has resisted all my attempts, and so this case remains among a bundle of other Knowsley mysteries that are bound together in a thick folder marked: Unknown.

Highway Invaders

This sea-girt country of ours is steeped in unfathomable mysteries. One of its earliest names was Albion, the Celtic word for 'white' because the first thing any approaching seaborne invader from the south saw of the so-called 'Misty Isles' was the ghostly white cliffs of Dover. Back in 325 BC, a Greek navigator named Pytheas was the first to call us Albion when he came to explore our shores to learn about the island that was producing the precious tin used in the bronze alloys of southern Europe's weapons. Pytheas was intrigued and a little intimidated by the Celts and their mysterious priests, the Druids, who carried out enigmatic mystical rites that are still cloaked in secrecy to this day.

Long before the druids there existed an even more enigmatic people who linked specific sites from the Orkneys, right across the British Isles to France with incredible alignments of gaunt cryptic standing stones of the type seen at Stonehenge (and, closer to home, in the ancient relics known as the Calder Stones). Compared to the ancient Geomancy-based religions of these peoples, Christianity is but a recent craze, and we know virtually nothing about these megalith builders – but their ghosts have allegedly been seen from time to time.

On the Monday morning of 3 August 1964, the Abbot family of Tuebrook set off for a bank holiday break at the country house of a relative near York. As chance would have it, as the Abbots joined the heavy traffic on the East Lancs road, the youngest member of the family, 11-year-old George Abbot, noticed his next door neighbour – a stern spinster he only knew as Miss Mince – driving behind them in her old car. Mr Abbot became increasingly irritable in the heat as the queue of holiday traffic crawled along. Then the car in front came to a sudden halt. Miss Mince's car gently bumped the rear end of the braking Ford Anglia in which the five Abbots were cooped up. A cacophony of disharmonious horns erupted. 'What's going on?' Mrs Abbot asked her husband, and he squinted through the windscreen and muttered: 'Those bloody Mods and Rockers by the looks of it.'

But the outlandish people invading the lanes of the East Lancs did not look like any Mod or Rocker Mrs Abbot had ever seen, because they were dressed in white toga-like robes and long flowing cloaks. They had hair longer than any Beatle, and wielded spears and swords. Some wore helmets and carried shields. These bizarre highway invaders were attacking the stationary cars with swords, axes and spears! One of the savages appeared at the side of the Abbots' car and peered in at George and his terrified older sister Tina. He had purple spirals which seemed to be tattooed into his face and grimaced at the frightened children. Mrs Abbot screamed as another figure tried to open the car door. Her husband revved the engine whilst it was still in neutral in an effort to scare off the primitive-looking visitors. It did the trick, and the two antiquated men jumped away from the car.

Mr Abbot then noticed another outdated 'warrior' striking the car in the next lane with an axe, but curiously, even though the axe-head seemed to strike the body of the car, no physical damage resulted, and because of the confusion caused by the extraordinary situation, as well as the screaming from Mrs Abbot and her daughter, Mr Abbot did not for a moment conclude that the sword and spear-wielding men were ghosts. He had boxed in his youth, and fancied his chances tackling the 'long-haired idiots' as he called the assailants, so he tried to get out of the car to tackle the man with the tattooed face who had scared his children. Mrs Abbot became even more hysterical and dragged her husband back as he opened the car door. 'Let go, I'll be alright!' he yelled. Just then Miss Mince behind sounded her horn and all the figures instantly vanished.

Mrs Abbot was still screaming, unaware at first that the mysterious figures had disappeared into thin air. Her husband began calming her down and the traffic started to move off, now that the people obstructing the cars had gone. Throughout the hundred-mile journey to the Yorkshire country house, the Abbots never stopped talking about the weird incident. Mrs Abbot thought the 'hooligans' were just Mods or Rockers who had decided to dress up; after all their had been a lot of trouble that year between the warring groups.

The Mods and Rockers had indeed made headlines that summer with clashes across the country, from Blackpool to Hastings, but Mr Abbot, who had seen gangs from both groups close up when he was working down south, knew that girls were always present in the disturbances, yet no girls had been amongst the strangely-dressed swordsmen on the East Lancs. He had an ominous feeling the figures were ghosts but not wishing to upset his children, he kept his thoughts to himself. When he did voice his theory that night in the privacy of their bedroom at the country house, his wife laughed and insisted that hoaxers had been at work, and now blamed students, who were well known for carrying out all sorts of rag-week stunts.

However, when the Abbots returned to Tuebrook a week later, Miss Mince bumped into Mrs Abbot at the cake shop and when the latter happened to joke about the 'attack' on the motorway, Miss Mince said the long-haired men had been the ghosts of some ancient tribe who might have mistaken modern cars for some sort of living beings. Miss Mince said she knew they were ghosts because when she sounded her horn, they vanished, and one of the men nearer to her car faded away into nothingness. The idea of dematerialisation spooked Mrs Abbot and she never mentioned the incident to her neighbour again.

Around the time of this apparent timeslip episode, very similar oddly-dressed long-haired figures were seen joining hands as they encircled a huge standing stone in a field near Ormskirk, but as the curious locals approached them, they vanished, along with the long tapering stone pillar.

THE MIRROR GHOST

Girls tend to remember dates, be it anniversaries or birthdays, but especially the dates when they first met a boyfriend, and 20-year-old Charm (short for Charmian) Woodley clearly recalled the day she first met John Bradford-Towson. Charm had been working as a waitress for a short while at Reece's Restaurant on Parker Street when she had first set eyes on the 21-year-old, and that date was 20 August 1963 – a Tuesday morning, Charm remembered. From the moment she had first looked at him there had been something there, some indefinable spark of attraction, and when he left Reece's, Charm felt so down, and longed to see him again. He came in for breakfast again on the following day, and the day after that, and by the Friday he had asked her out.

The first thing he bought Charm was a 45 single of *Bad to Me* by Billy J Kramer and The Dakotas from NEMs record store on Whitechapel. He had heard her singing that song on that Tuesday as he watched her for the first time from behind a copy of the *Mersey Beat* newspaper. The second thing John bought his love was a red Dansette radio, because Charm loved to listen to the pop charts and all of the latest songs. John worked as a trainee electrician for a big retail store in town and the money wasn't that good, and yet he was always spending what little he had on Charm. It sounded like a cliché but the couple were really made for each other, and now months after their paths in life crossed, John proposed to her on the ferry to New Brighton. The wedding was to be in the summer of 1964. They moved into a bed-sit on Upper Parliament Street, and one rainy evening, John was gazing into the flames in the fire-grate when he suddenly said, 'If I died, would you miss me?'

'You morbid sod, of course I would,' Charm replied, adding: 'I'd kill myself to be with you. I couldn't go on without you.'

'Don't ever do that, love,' John whispered as he kissed Charm's earlobe, 'I'd want you to be happy and meet someone else.' But she squeezed him and said, 'No, I'd have to be with you; just you and no one else ... ever.'

Thunder rolled in the skies of south Liverpool, and John hugged Charm and said, 'Well I'm planning on living forever, so don't worry.'

But that November John was involved in an horrific car crash in Wales. He was taken to Walton Hospital where his condition was described as touch and go. Charm, as you can imagine, was in a dreadful state; hardly ate or slept and kept playing *Bad to Me* and always sobbed when she heard the line that ran: 'but I know you won't leave me 'cos you told me so, and I've no intention of letting you go'. Charm was constantly at John's bedside in Walton Hospital, squeezing his hand and willing him to live. Then one day, Tina, Charm's friend, called with the devastating news that John had died.

The world ended for Charm there and then.

That evening, she saw John's ghost in the mirror of her dresser in the bed-sit. 'Come with me,' he called out to her, holding out his hand. 'John?' Charm's tears rolled down her face.

The ghost told her how lovely it was 'on the other side'. And then he told her exactly how to end her life so she could be with him, but on her way to fetch a knife from the kitchen, she saw the landlord open the front door to reveal John standing there. It had all been a terrible misunderstanding. Tina had asked about John and the nurse had said he had 'gone' – meaning he'd been discharged, but she had taken it to mean he had died. In fact, John had made a miraculous recovery and had been in such a rush to see his fiancee, he had discharged himself from the hospital.

John embraced his sobbing sweetheart and now she found herself crying tears of joy. She looked into his eyes and asked if it was just a cruel dream, and John, who was rather choked up, assured her it wasn't. 'I was in the arms of the angels, Charm,' he said, and told her how he believed they had let him come back to earth because he missed her so much.

Then Charm recalled the strange vision of John in her mirror. Who then, or what, had been the thing in the mirror that had urged her to commit suicide? John immediately dashed upstairs, and every step of the way, Charm urged him not to go, because she believed something evil was up there in that mirror. He reached the bed-sit, and found no one in the room – but the mirror where Charm had seen John's doppelganger was cracked straight down the middle.

The couple moved out that day.

Cleared by a Medium

Quite a few decades ago, in the 1970s, there was a certain well-known clothes shop on Liverpool's Church Street, where something very intriguing took place. It began one autumnal late morning in 1977, when Catherine, a pretty 19-year-old from Old Swan, was summoned to the office of the store's manager, Mr Phillips. Mrs Skellin, who had worked at the store for nearly 30 years, was the one who told young Catherine with a smirk that she was wanted upstairs by Mr Phillips. Catherine had only been working in the shop for a month, and she had been very punctual – getting to her workplace early each morning and striving to serve every customer as professionally as she could. So why did Mr Phillips want to see her? As Catherine left her counter in menswear, Mrs Skellin took her place, and all of the other employees on that floor watched the teenager heading anxiously for the stairs. Old Mr Reynolds immediately went over to Mrs Skellin to ask what the problem was.

'Oh, that's not for me to say,' Skellin replied meekly, looking down at the controls of the till with a glimmer of subdued excitement in her eyes. 'It's a private matter between the girl and Mr Phillips, and if we need to know anything I'm sure Mr Phillips will tell us.'

'You don't like Catherine, do you?' said Mr Reynolds bluntly. He was known by all in the shop as a no-nonsense man who spoke his mind.

'What do you mean?' Skellin scrunched up her face and shot a look at Reynolds that was halfway between perplexity and scorn.

'Oh, we've all seen the way you're carrying on,' said Reynolds whipping off his spectacles and placing the arms of his glasses in his mouth as he nodded, 'just because she's a lovely young thing. It was the same with Judy last year. You drove that poor girl to hand in her cards in the end.'

'How dare you ...!' Mrs Skellin gritted her dentures and her eyes seemed to burn into Reynolds.

A customer six feet away from the contentious duo stopped

browsing for gloves and enjoyed the lively barney that was brewing.

'You were young once, Mrs Skellin, and I remember when you first came to work here,' Reynolds reminisced, 'and old Mrs Sloane didn't take to you, did she? Isn't it funny how jealousy repeats itself?'

And Mr Reynolds turned and walked back to his own counter. All of the other staff members turned their faces to Mrs Skellin, who was probably blushing beneath her many layers of foundation.

Meanwhile, upstairs in Mr Phillips' office, there was a single faint rap at the door.

'Come in!' Phillips shouted, and the large mahogany door opened slowly and Catherine peeped around it, her pallid face full of worry. 'Sir?' she muttered.

Phillips looked over the top of his spectacles and gave a brief nod towards the empty chair on the other side of his huge well-kept desk.

Catherine gently closed the door and walked with faltering steps to the chair. Her palms felt sweaty against the armrests of the chair as she sat down.

Phillips looked at the white typewritten sheet on his inkblotter before swiping off his glasses and looking at Catherine with a pair of accusatory squinting eyes. 'You started here just over four weeks ago, and in that time, there have been a number of thefts near your counter.'

Thefts? The word pulsated in Catherine's chest and in the veins of her forehead. She felt breathless.

'Now, no one is accusing you of stealing these items.' And Phillips picked up the white sheet and handed it to Catherine. She began to read the list of stolen items as her heart palpitated. 'One Ben Sherman Shirt, size L, 15/09/77. Three ties 16/09/77. One grey Maxi Skirt, size 12 ...'

Phillips coughed to clear his voice and cast a stern look right into Catherine's blinking eyes. 'You will see from the grand total at the foot of this list that these thefts have cost this store seventy-three pounds, which is a very serious matter. I will of course have to inform the police.'

'I haven't taken anything, Mr Phillips, on my gran's grave, I swear I haven't,' Catherine seemed close to bursting into tears.

'Your late grandmother is beside the point,' her boss said coldly, his icy blue-grey eyes fixed on the sheet that was now quivering in her shaking hands. 'I cannot prove you have taken these items, but does it not seem odd that all of the purloined articles have been taken from places around or near to your corner of the store?'

Catherine cried at last, and she put the paper down on the desk and wiped her tears as she looked at Phillips, shaking her head, insisting she was not a thief.

Phillips snatched back the white sheet. 'If there are any further thefts, I will not hesitate to call in the police, and should you be charged, you will not only become unemployable, you may even face a jail sentence.'

'I don't know what to say,' Catherine sobbed. 'I haven't done anything.'

'Then good day,' said Mr Phillips curtly.

Catherine rose from the chair, dumbfounded and confused at being suspected of the thefts. She backed away towards the door, blundered into its handle, and let herself out. When she went back downstairs, Mr Reynolds immediately went over to her. He saw her red eyes and tear-smeared mascara.

Mrs Skellin was about to go over to her, but Mr Reynolds took her by the hand and led her towards the staff room door.

'Where are you taking her?' Mrs Skellin shouted over to Reynolds, who raised his palm to her without facing her.

'For elevenses,' he said.

'Mr Reynolds! This is most inconsiderate ...' Mrs Skellin was protesting, but Reynolds quickly ushered Catherine into the staff room and slammed the door behind him.

In the staff room, Catherine told Mr Reynolds about the thefts amounting to seventy-three pounds and how the manager had accused her of being behind them.

'What?' Reynolds recoiled, pausing to stir the girl's coffee.

'I swear on my life, Mr Reynolds, I have never stolen anything in my life,' Catherine almost started to cry again, and dabbed her watering eyes with a napkin.

'I believe you, Catherine,' Reynolds told the distressed teen, 'so please don't be upset. We do get what we call 'inventory shrinkage' due to shoplifters. This is a major city, and we do get professional thieves in here. I've told Phillips to put in closed circuit television cameras but he won't have it. Why on earth would he accuse you? Has someone been down his ears?'

'What do you mean?' Catherine was intrigued.

'Well, just between you and me, Mrs Skellin seems very jealous of you,' Reynolds said frankly as he slid a small plate of biscuits across the table towards Catherine. 'I wouldn't put it past her to put your name in the hat.'

'Why, is she like that?' Catherine asked, 'She seemed alright at first when I started here.'

'Some women can deal with age, but some women ... and well, men too for that matter; well, they see younger people as competition.'

'Do you think I should just leave?' Catherine wondered openly.

'No, you're not letting her win,' the avuncular Reynolds leaned over and placed his hand on Catherine's left shoulder and squeezed it. 'We'll get to the bottom of this one, don't you worry!'

On the following day, Catherine was early for work as usual. The store opened at 9am and she was on the premises 15 minutes before that. Reynolds winked over at her from the sportswear section, then shot a distant inconsiderate look at Mrs Skellin, who was at her usual post in the lingerie section tucked away in a diagonal corner of the floor. Lingerie was temporarily on the ground floor because of the extensive decorating taking place on the second floor.

Mr Reynolds was watching Catherine's corner like a hawk, determined to catch any shoplifter red-handed, and the same corner was also being watched by Mrs Skellin, who dreamed of catching the innocent little teenager in the act of thievery. Catherine was also on the alert for shoplifters, and hoped that by catching one she could prove her innocence.

At 10.20am, an eccentric-looking woman in her fifties came into the store, and began to browse the ladies' scarves and gloves. She wore a mackintosh, a floral skirt just below the knees, and on her head she had a pointed green hat with a yellow feather in it, and one of the staff members, young Edmund, who worked under the supervision of Mr Reynolds in sportswear, sniggered, 'Hey! Get William Tell,' to his supervisor.

'Shut up, Edmund,' Reynolds said suppressing a smile.

The oddly-dressed woman suddenly stopped ranging through the scarves and turned to face Catherine. Catherine didn't notice her staring at first, but as soon as she did she became uneasy. She smiled awkwardly at the middle-aged shopper, who then came over to the counter. Reynolds and Edmund watched her and wondered what she was going to say to Catherine. 'You're like a lighthouse, you know?' she said.

'Sorry?' Catherine didn't have a clue what she meant.

The woman saw that the teen was baffled and tried to explain. 'You're broadcasting all sorts of horrible, negative things from that pretty little head of yours. You're very sad, aren't you?'

Catherine found herself nodding to the question. The woman held the girl's hands in hers and said, 'Don't you worry about anything; it will all turn out alright.'

'That's good,' Catherine said, blushing slightly.

There was a pause as the woman continued to tighten her grip around Catherine's tiny hands. 'Oh my, oh my, oh my!' The woman looked around the floor, and then she seemed to set eyes on something no one else could see. She let go of Catherine's hands and went to a display where an array of tee shirts was laid out. The woman began to talk to herself as a bemused Mr Reynolds and Edmund looked on.

Then one of the tee shirts seemed to fling itself off the display and on to the floor, which wiped the smiles off the faces of Mr Reynolds and Edmund. Mrs Skellin left her counter and walked gingerly over to the woman, believing her to be unhinged.

'You are not allowed here any more!' the woman shouted, aiming her outburst at something about seven feet above the tee shirt table.

Customers were startled out of their aimless browsing and turned to look at the source of the disturbance.

'You have almost had this poor girl sacked because of your stupid games!' the woman in the William Tell hat cried out.

More tee shirts were hurled off the table and Mrs Skellin threw her hands up to her face in shock.

'Bring them back or by the God above us I will send you to Hell!' the woman bellowed, and her face flushed red.

A spray of some liquid hit the woman in the face. It came out of mid-air, and she swore when it hit her. And then a bundle of clothes, all soaking wet, slopped down on to the shop floor. A grey maxi skirt, a Ben Sherman shirt, ties, socks, a jacket ...

The woman, who subsequently gave her name as Marjorie, went to Catherine and told the trembling girl that the spirit of a woman who had worked in the store a long time ago (back in the 1920s, when she had died) had been snatching items with the wicked intention of laying the blame on her. Marjorie called the entity Gloria, and said the spirit was jealous of Catherine because of two things: her beauty, and the fact that she was alive. This claim really filled Catherine with fear, and she was almost ready to quit her job, but then worried that Mr Phillips would see her departure as confirmation of her guilt, so she stuck around.

At first her boss said he did not believe in ghosts and said some elaborate hoax was being perpetrated on the staff. Marjorie told him she was a medium who had been able to see the inhabitants of the spirit world for as long as she could remember, but her talk of the 'invisible society of ghosts all around us' was not taken seriously by the manager.

However, around a week after the alleged apport of sodden clothes which seemed to appear out of thin air in the store, Mr Phillips came down to the ground floor from his office one late afternoon with a noticeably pale face. He told Mrs Skellin that all of the furniture in his office had just been 'jumping around'. Phillips began to visit the staff more and more often as the weeks went by, as if he was afraid to stay in his office alone, and in the January of the following year he took early retirement after suffering a mild heart attack, which, he later claimed, was brought on by the appearance of a 'smoky figure' in his office.

Catherine eventually left the store and went to work in Lewis's for a while before she finally found a well-paid job in retail down in London. The ghost that stole items is still seen occasionally but the firm that operates in the haunted building nowadays does not deal in clothes. Female giggling has been heard in the stock room of this firm, and on one occasion in 2002, the wall of the stockroom was given a new layer of plaster, and in the morning when the plasterers came to complete their work in another part of the building, they saw small handprints all over the newly-plastered wall.

I have researched this case and as of yet, I have been unable to find out the identity of the female ghost.

SHORE LEAVE

In the late 1950s, a young sailor in full Royal naval attire, calling himself Tommo, a nickname derived from his surname Thompson, came into a certain well-known pub in Liverpool city centre. He stood among the drinkers at the bar, trying to get served, when the beautiful red-haired barmaid, Rosy, suddenly asked him what he wanted. The sailor seemed surprised and a little amused at being noticed at last, and said, 'Oh, I'll order in a minute, love. What happened to Joan?'

'Joan?' Rosy asked, looking perplexed. 'There's no one here of that name.'

'She worked here just a year ago,' said Tommo, with sadness in his clear baby-blue eyes, 'And I promised her I'd come back and marry her.'

Rosy shrugged, 'Sorry, I've only been working here a few months. What can I get you?'

The landlord, Mr Connor, a shrewd streetwise square-shouldered man, asked the sailor what ship he had come off.

'The *Hood*,' Tommo replied proudly, then lifted his eyes to the ceiling and added: '*HMS Hood.*'

'Oh, really? And when are you due back at sea, lad?' Connor asked, puffing on a Senior Service cigarette as he pulled the pump handle.

The sailor grew annoyed, 'Why do they all say that as soon as we get shore leave – "when are you going back?" – I've only just landed here!'

'Alright, son, just asking, now what're you having?' Connor retorted, 'You can see we're busy.'

'Pint of mild,' mumbled Tommo and immediately started complaining about the 'racket' coming from the juke-box. 'Who *is* that?' he asked Rosy, and she told him it was Bill Haley and his Comets, but Tommo gritted his teeth, saying it wasn't music, it was just a noise. He asked Rosy if she could put on some Glenn Miller, and the barmaid said, 'It's not up to me, it's up to the drinkers.'

'Lime Street's changed, hasn't it?' Tommo suddenly remarked. 'Not one of the ladies wants to know me; used to attract them like flies when I came to town with me wages in me tail. Cases aren't they?'

Mr Connor clunked down the freshly-drawn pint of mild on the bar counter, and as the sailor went to delve into his purse, an old man confronted him. 'Why're you telling them you're on the *Hood*, eh?' An evident volcano of hatred and anger was simmering in the oldster's eyes and he shook with rage. Mr Connor, in the midst of the bustle of the pub, noticed this and Tommo was taken aback by the old man's question and obvious anger.

'Think its funny do you?' the old man raged. 'Have you ever really been to sea?'

'Course I have, dad,' Tommo told him, 'just come back from the Denmark Strait! Fourteen hundred of our lads died. I'm lucky to be here.'

'My son died on that ship, you ... you bloody phoney!' said the old man, and tried to throw a punch, but Mr Connor's huge hand shot across the counter and seized his fist. He then advised the sailor to 'Beat it'. But another drinker, a man in his forties with an eye-patch, had also started taking Tommo to task about his alleged service on *HMS Hood*. He asked him who commanded the battlecruiser, and Tommo correctly answered that it was Captain Kerr, but the sailor now found himself surrounded by a hostile circle of sceptical drinkers hurling insults at him.

Tommo suddenly turned to the barmaid Rosy, and with a look of great sadness in his eyes, said: 'If you do happen to see Joan, tell her I love her and meant what I said.'

Rosy nodded. She felt so sorry for the harassed sailor as he turned with his head bowed and headed for the door, but Mr Connor, said the 'sailor' was a con-man because *HMS Hood* had been destroyed in 1941 during the Second World War.

'Are you sure?' said Rosy.

'Course I'm bleedin' sure ... blown to smithereens over fifteen years ago, when that con-merchant would have been about ten years old!' and as Connor spoke his cigarette levered up and down between his lips.

'Lying bastard,' said an old voice amongst the drinkers, and out of the cloud of cigarette and pipe smoke hanging blue in the shafts of sunlight coming through the window, another aged voice said: 'How do these people think they can get away with it?'

Minutes later, an old regular known as Sinnot came into the pub and said to Connor: 'Hey, did you hear what happened today in the Baltic Fleet?'

'Go on,' Connor replied, without even looking up at the old man as he studied the racing pages of the *Daily Mirror* on the bar counter.

'Five sailors came in, claiming they'd come off *HMS Hood*.' The barman said to them, 'You must all be ghosties then,' and the five lads all bowed their heads and vanished into thin air.'

At this, Connor's face lifted and he turned to look at Rosy, who was gawping in shock and disbelief at her employer.

'You hear some tales and tripe in alehouses but Georgie O'Hare's a red-hot Catholic, never lied in his life, and he was there,' Sinnot told Connor, 'And he swore on his youngest's life that these five young lads just faded away in front of him.'

It is said that a few years later, the story of the ghostly sailors from the *Hood* reached the ears of a woman named Joan, and she confirmed that one of the brave men off the battlecrusier had indeed promised to marry her as soon as he came ashore – but he had tragically been killed on the ship. Love is a very powerful emotion, and I wonder – is it possible that an unfulfilled promise of marriage somehow brought a young sailor back from his watery grave?

THE WAVERTREE THING

I had heard about the entity featured in this chapter so many times over the years but until July 2012 I had not heard a report from anyone who had encountered it firsthand and at close quarters. Mick Smethurst, who is 70 at the time of writing, now lives in Cheshire, but in his youth he lived in Wavertree, and it was he who related to me his intriguing encounters with an unknown creature.

On the Thursday night of 3 October 1963, at around 1.20am, a huge harvest moon hung over Liverpool, and 21-year-old Mick Smethurst left his girlfriend's house on Wavertree's Cecil Street and headed for his home on Garmoyle Road, where his mother would be waiting to make him his ritual supper of scallops – not the shellfish of that name, but thick fried slices of parboiled spuds: a delicious prospect to young Mick on such a cold night. He knew Wavertree's entries and back-alleyways (colloquially called 'jiggers' in Liverpool) like the back of his hand, and as he wended his way home down the long entry off Grosvenor Road, he saw something moving out of the corner of his eye. A weird unearthly-looking figure was peeping at him from behind the rounded wall of the entry. It was well over six feet in height, and its head, torso and limbs were skeletally thin. The elongated head was almost the same shape as a beer-pump handle, only a bit thicker, and the entity reminded Mick of one of those mannikin artists use as models. In the bright moonlight, the thing had a greenish cast to it, but no visible facial features. Mick felt a cold shudder when he realised he was seeing the thing his kid sister Mo claimed to have seen a week ago at the mouth of an alleyway off

Rathbone Road as she got off the bus after visiting her friend at around 10pm. No one had believed 'Little Mo' of course.

Mick quickly retraced his steps back down the alleyway and decided to go up Lawrence Road instead. Mick told his mother about the 'thing' and she told him that lots of people – including her daughter Mo – had seen the 'bogeyman' in places ranging from Smithdown Road to Wavertree High Street. Even the police had chased him, and she said the joker would be laughing on the other side of his face when he was caught.

'There are some very peculiar people knocking about nowadays, and they get their ideas from all these stupid films on the telly. That box puts ideas into their heads,' Mrs Smethurst opined, nodding gravely at the television set in the corner of the room.

'Mam, I saw it, and I can definitely tell you it wasn't someone acting the goat,' Mick said, peppering his scallops. 'It was like something from ... I dunno ... outer space.'

'Oh don't talk so daft,' his mother snapped. 'It's someone messing about, that's all.'

Mick shook his head and tried to enjoy his supper but couldn't forget the faceless entity. That night he lay in bed, trying to work out what he'd seen, and wondering if the thing had followed him home. He got out of bed, sneaked over to the window, and peered through the net curtains. The street was dark and silent, and thankfully there was nothing sinister lurking there.

On the following Saturday he took his girlfriend Rita to the Grosvenor pub (on Wavertree's Grosvenor Road, of course), and at around 11pm he went with her to her house on Cecil Street until her parents came home at half-past midnight. He then went home again, and this time he saw two men around his age standing in the shadows of the entry on Grosvenor Road. Eyeing them suspiciously, Mick shouted, 'Gorra light lads?' But it turned out that the two men were not muggers or burglars, but two students named Spencer and Phil who had also seen the 'Wavertree Thing' on several occasions over the course of the previous week, and who were at that moment lying in wait for it. Mick shared his cigarettes with the lads and together they patrolled Wavertree as far as Picton Clock, where several like-minded people told them that the 'thing' had just been seen in nearby Hunters Lane, chasing a cat. Witnesses said the entity sometimes moved so fast their eyes couldn't follow it, and it never made any noise when it ran.

A few days after this, Mick was drinking in the Prince Alfred pub on Wavertree's High Street when two excited lads burst into the premises, telling their friends that the Thing was at large once again round the corner on Chestnut Grove. Mick and his friends followed the animated youth to Chestnut Grove, where a number of people, many of them residents of all ages, were standing in a knot at the top of the street. Most of them claimed to have just seen the Thing run off towards the High Street. Mick and about a dozen people went in pursuit of the creepy entity, and upon pouring out on to the High Street, met a number of people who said the emaciated figure had bolted down Sandown Lane, and it was on this lane that Mick and a group of other pursuers actually saw it stooping down behind an old car, apparently peeping at them. Mick urged everyone present not to rush at the Thing. 'Just hang on here,' he advised, 'and see if it comes out,' but three teenagers couldn't contain themselves and ran towards the car, upon which the Thing flew off down the lane at a phenomenal speed and vanished into the night. That was the last time Mick set eyes on the enigmatic entity.

The Wavertree Thing – whatever it was – was seen sporadically for a few more months, then vanished into obscurity – but the question on everyone's lips is, will it ever return?

LIVERPOOL'S LITTLE PEOPLE

Way back when the Domesday Book listed Wavertree as Wavretreu, when Allerton was known as Alre Tune, and Childwall, Cildeuuelle, six mysterious megaliths still guarded the tomb of an ancient unknown personage in a mound near to what is now the district of Calderstones. The people of that bygone era held an unquestioning belief in the supernatural, even though they could not understand the lore and laws of the occult, just as scientists today cannot fully understand the topsy-turvy laws of Quantum Physics – but the Norse, Celtic, Anglo-Saxon and Norman peoples of our ancient settlements respected and acknowledged the occult, and magic, and many of them were in tune with forces we have lost touch with.

All the clues are around us, in mysterious tracts of land such as Bloody Acre, which is traditionally deemed to be out of bounds to man, woman or child, for reasons we have long forgotten. There are telluric forces and lines of power criss-crossing our land, between enigmatic standing stones (like the Robin Hood Stone of Booker Avenue), and these forces centre on such landmarks as Camp Hill, which forms one of the Seven Hills of Liverpool.

When Christianity reached our shores, the Church deliberately built places of worship atop these hills and hijacked many of the dates of the old calendar by stamping their own holy days upon them, so Easter, a time of fertility rites and the Spring Equinox, became associated with the Resurrection of Christ, and 25 December, when the old priests, Druids and wizards observed the Winter Equinox, became Christmas. Halloween was similarly sabotaged by the Church and mixed up with All Saints Day – but the 'old religion' refuses to die, and more and more people are rediscovering it. Even today, in certain parts of Ireland, civil engineers will refuse to build on 'fairy mounds' – ancient hillocks and such that are rumoured to have historical associations with the 'Little People'. Motorways have been built in curves around these mounds rather than go through them, as all sorts of bad luck – even death – have been known to result when they have been disturbed.

The people of this land held a similar respect for the Little People and other supernatural beings until 597 AD, when over-zealous friars, limetours, Christian exorcists and missionaries landed at Canterbury with St Augustine to convert the British to Christianity. Nothing short of an ideological war was waged by the Holy Invaders against people we would now term Wiccans. The witches' craft was branded as the work of the Devil, because the male-dominated

Church didn't want the witches, who were mostly female, to have any sway over the people, and of course, centuries of persecution began, ending in witch-hunts and executions. Some freethinkers did not succumb to the new religious cult from Rome, and continued to acknowledge the mysterious forces of nature and the supernatural, and our neck of the woods – Liverpool – was no exception.

Even today there are many covens and occultists based in this area, and this city, and Merseyside as a whole, is a very mysterious place. Take for example, the many sightings of the Little People alone in Liverpool. The most well-known incident of this kind took place in Kensington in the summer of 1964, when hundreds of people, young and old, saw little men, some just eight inches tall, dressed in strange red and green clothes, and pointed hats, playing on the bowling green off Jubilee Drive. That summer, more sightings came pouring in of Little People who had been seen in Sefton Park, Calderstones Park, Abercromby Park, Bowring Park, Allerton Golf Course, and even the graveyard of St Chads in Kirkby. 'Leprechaun Mania', as it was labelled by the *Liverpool Echo*, became as widespread and uncontrollable as Beatlemania, with police being drafted in to control mobs of adults and children equipped with fishing nets and jam jars converging on the parks of the city to hopefully capture one of the little folk.

Earlier still, back in 1957, there was a smaller outbreak of sightings of 'fairies' and the Little People in Mossley Hill. Most of the sightings of five-inch-tall men dressed in green coats and pointed black hats were regarded as silly rumours at first, but many people reported seeing these beings, and I interviewed a few of the witnesses at the studios of BBC Radio Merseyside some years ago. One witness, named Louise, was 68 when I interviewed her in 1997, but back in 1957, when she was in her twenties, Louise was a down-to-earth housewife living in a semi on Rose Lane.

One summer afternoon in August of that year, Louise was in her back garden, taking the washing off the line, when she heard what sounded like the faint laughter of children. The young housewife put the washing in a basket, and looked about her. She could see no children anywhere – and then she noticed what she thought was a doll of some sort, standing on the top of her fence. But on closer inspection Louise realised it was not a doll, because it moved in a very lifelike manner. Then she saw three other little men, all wearing green attire, running along the fence, and one of these tiny figures shouted something too faint to be intelligible, and jumped on to the washing line. Louise dashed inside and locked the kitchen door behind her.

Minutes later, as Louise was still wondering if she was going insane, there was a heavy knocking at the front door. It was her neighbour, Mrs Jones. She had also seen the little people running round in her own garden.

These same little men in green were seen in Calderstones Park weeks later, and then the sightings died down and there were no further reports.

The following story was told to me in 1998 by a reader who had come to talk to me at a booksigning.

One frosty February evening in 1972, 32-year-old Marianne looked at the clock on the mantelpiece of her friend Carol's living room and saw it was 9.45pm. 'God, is that the time?' she gasped. Quickly stubbing out her cigarette in the ashtray she leapt to her feet. She had been so busy gossiping with her friend, she had lost all track of time, and she knew husband Alan at their home off Lodge Lane would be cursing her now because he'd have put the children to bed and read the youngest the mandatory bedtime story or two – and she had also forgotten to pick up a bottle of Cheerio sauce at the shop round the corner from Carol's house on Belmont Road. Marianne left the house and hurried to the shop, but found it closed, which was odd, as it was usually open till 10pm. Then Marianne saw what time it really was when she passed a pub and glanced through the window at its clock – nearly 11pm! Carol's wind-up clock had stopped at 9.45pm. Alan would be doubly cross over something as petty as his 'stop-out wife' (as he called her) forgetting the bottle of Cheerio sauce, which he liberally poured on everything – even his nightly cheese on toast.

Marianne waited at the bus stop for the number 26 to take her home, and regretted not wearing her scarf and gloves as Alan had suggested, because the cold was biting; the icy breeze had a razor edge to it which made her eyes water. Marianne stamped her feet and saw a bus in the distance, but it turned the corner on to Breck Road. Time always seems to drag when you're waiting for a bus, but Marianne felt there was also an unusual quietness about this night, and the full moon lent a spooky aspect to the hush. She realised that there wasn't a soul about except for a few figures she could just make out in the distance beyond the junction at Sheil Road.

Marianne suddenly heard faint laughter somewhere in the distance. She listened – yes, she could definitely hear distant children's laughter, but as she tried to get a fix on where it was coming from, a huge red Regent Oil Atkinson articulated tanker thundered past, drowning out the chortling sounds. Then the heavy, unnatural silence descended once again, and Marianne heard the strangest music, if that was what you could call the sounds coming from somewhere close by – a thumping drum, plus a melody that sounded as if it was coming from a speeded-up flautist, and a rhythmic metallic gong-like tone like nothing she had ever heard. Then she saw something green and faintly luminous, like the glow-in-the-dark radiance of numerals on a watch, out of the corner of her eye. She turned to glance at the greenish gleaming object and saw two things dancing to the unearthly racket. They were two little green men in pointed hats of some sort, about three feet from her feet, and about a foot in from the kerb. They were around ten inches tall, about the size of her son's Action Man doll.

Marianne was dumbstruck for a moment, then let out a little yelp, and then a scream. The figures stopped dancing and they began to swear in coarse language at Marianne in tinny-sounding voices. Their little faces became contorted with hatred and they waved their fists at Marianne who actually felt her teeth chatter with fear as the little green men walked towards her, and she reacted by blindly backing away into the road. A car horn suddenly blasted, and tyres screeched. Marianne turned and saw a car halt just a few feet away from her. By sheer coincidence, she noticed that the man behind the wheel was her next-door neighbour, 60-year-old Mr Parkes, and he suddenly recognised her. Marianne turned to look back at the spot on the pavement where the little men had been advancing towards her, but to her relief found that they had vanished, and in a complete daze she got into her neighbour's car.

'That was a close one, Mari,' Mr Parkes joked, but she just sat there staring at the pavement.

'Sorry, what?' Marianne asked looking at Mr Parkes.

'You going home then, Mari?' Parkes asked. 'You okay, love?'

'You won't believe what I just saw ...' Marianne began, but her neighbour interrupted her by saying, 'I saw them too ... like little leprechaun things.'

Marianne shot a look of amazement to her neighbour. 'Did you really see them as well?'

Mr Parkes nodded as he put the car into gear and moved off. 'I was going to call on my sister ... she hasn't been too good ... but I think it's a bit too late now, so I'll take you home.' He did a perfect u-turn and headed down Belmont Road towards Sheil Road.

'What were they?' Marianne asked, as if her neighbour should know. She was so glad that he had seen them as otherwise she would have doubted her own sanity.

'I haven't a clue, Mari,' he admitted, then added, 'I saw them as I came up from Sheil Road in the distance as a tiny green point of light, and then as I got nearer, I still couldn't make them out until I was about 30 yards away, and then I thought they were dolls of some sort. Then you backed out into my path.'

'They swore at me. Their faces were horrible, so full of hatred. What the hell are they?'

Marianne and her neighbour agreed it was best to say nothing to anyone about the weird little entities, as people would only think they were nuts. But Marianne found that she just had to tell Carol though, and her friend said the so-called leprechauns had probably been dolls or puppets someone had been manipulating from behind a bush, but Marianne said there had been no bushes anywhere near that bus stop on Belmont Road and by no stretch of the imagination was there any place a hidden puppeteer could have operated them from.

Never again did Marianne stay late at her friend's home, for fear of another meeting with the hostile little green men.

Many years later, in the 1990s, when Marianne first heard the new techno dance music being played on radio and Television, she realised it sounded exactly like the music she had heard the 'leprechauns' dancing to 20 years before on that night in 1972, which only deepens this mystery.

Is it possible that the little men in their strange attire were time travellers from some future age, dancing to what would have been vintage dance music to them? What purpose would such a trip to 1972 even serve? Or were the miniature men from some other reality? We'll probably never know. There have been sightings of the Little Folk all over the world, in every era, but just what these Lilliputian beings actually are remains a mystery. Maybe you should go and have a look at a secluded spot at the bottom of your garden – perhaps there really are fairies there ...

DISAPPEARING DOHERTY

I am not here, this is not real,
Let go of now, let go of now
I am not me, you are not you,
Let the world go, let it all go

The Mantra of Letting Go

On 25 April,1967, the death of 40-year-old Soviet Cosmonaut Colonel Vladimir Komarov was reported all over the world. Komarov was the first human confirmed to have died on a space mission, and he met his untimely end whilst returning to earth from an orbital flight after the parachute of his spacecraft became entangled at a height of seven kilometres. As Komarov plummeted four miles to his death, his last thoughts were probably of his wife Valentina and his little daughter Ira. The voice of the Premier of the Soviet Union, Aleksei Kosygin, came blaring through the doomed cosmonaut's headphones, assuring Komarov that Russia was proud of him.

Months before this tragedy, in January of the same year, US astronauts Gus Grissom, Ed White and Roger Chaffee died in an horrific fire in the command module of Apollo 1 during a training exercise on a launch pad at Cape Canaveral. The fire of unknown origin in the pure oxygen atmosphere of the cabin had been so intense, the spacesuits of Grissom and White had melted and fused together. The Apollo 11 astronauts Neil Armstrong and Buzz Aldrin, later left an Apollo 1 mission patch on the lunar surface before returning to earth from the Moon in July 1969.

On the day space pioneer Vladimir Komarov's death was reported, 25 April 1967, a Liverpool pioneer of space and time was allegedly carrying out a very controversial experiment. He was a hippie known as 'Disappearing Doherty' because he was said to be able to 'project himself' out of the present and into the past or future. This sounds far-fetched, I admit, and initially I was very sceptical of the claims surrounding Stephen Doherty, but having researched this intriguing case, I am now not so sure.

In March 2003, during my weekly slot on the Billy Butler Show, I talked of time travel, and during the broadcast I jokingly asked any time travellers who happened to be listening to call the station. A mysterious caller named Ken rang Radio Merseyside and left a message for me. Within this message the listener predicted the death (by heart attack) of actor Adam Faith, 48 hours before it took place. Billy Butler checked with the BBC station's newsroom, but Adam Faith was alive and well and appearing in a play that day. Two days later the actor died of a massive heart attack.

I received several intriguing emails and letters, all unsigned, from a person who had an uncanny knowledge of future events, including an accurate prediction of a tidal wave in the Indian Ocean in 'late 2004' – and of course an infamous Tsunami killed 225,000 people on Boxing Day of that year. A letter predicting the death of Pope John

Paul II in 2005 was also sent to me, and the writer of this missive hinted that he had sent the email predicting the Tsunami. Not long after this I was appearing as a guest on the Pete Price phone-in when an elderly woman called the show and asked me to visit her. She had an incredible tale to tell me about a man she had known who could travel through time. This man was Stephen Doherty, and I will herewith relate his alleged travels into our decade and beyond, and the things he said he saw which might horrify and intrigue you.

In 1967, Stephen Doherty allegedly discovered how to travel through time whilst meditating in his attic lodgings on Aigburth Drive in the shadow of Belem Tower, Sefton Park. An Indian mystic named Tarak, who Stephen had happened to meet at an assembly of the so-called Society of Initiates at a Hope Street lodge in 1966, had trained Doherty to mentally and physically 'let go' of the present. This unusual form of meditation is akin to sensory deprivation, whereby a blindfolded and ear-muffed person is suspended inside a soundproof flotation tank and cut off from all the distracting stimuli of the external world. A person subjected to such isolation hears, sees and smells nothing, virtually feels nothing, and begins to hallucinate.

In 1967, Stephen Doherty eliminated environmental stimuli in a more effective manner by sheer well-honed willpower as he sat cross-legged, centre carpet in his attic apartment. He looked every inch the hippie with his long hair and psychedelic attire, but had never indulged in drugs to expand his mind – Tarak's Method did that for him. Sitting nearby, watching this esoteric exercise, was 40-year-old Juliet, the landlady of the house where Stephen lodged. According to Juliet, Stephen became faintly transparent as he meditated, then vanished altogether. He reappeared, bedraggled and exhausted on a rainy Aigburth Drive later that night, with a soggy newspaper, which, on closer inspection, proved to be a copy of *The Times*, dated Friday, 12 August 1892.

Stephen had an incredible tale to tell. As he had meditated in the attic he had found himself in a black timeless void. Something told him this was the 'Gulf' between the living and the dead. Countless pale faces appeared in rows that surrounded him. Most of the faces stared open-eyed with blank expressions, but a few had their eyes closed. Stephen addressed the voice of the unseen entity with a question: 'Where is this?' and was told: 'This is the place where most of the dead go; they have no minds here and so they don't care about anything, as there is no yesterday or tomorrow.' Stephen willed himself away from that place of dread and found himself sitting on a cold pavement under an old fashioned lamppost. There was a flickering flame in the lantern at the top of the lamppost, and its light revealed an eerily quainter Aigburth Drive than the one he had left behind in 1967. Then the hansom cab trundled past, and Doherty realised he'd gone back into either Victorian or Edwardian times.

He called at a house with a plaque which read 'Torrisholme' on its frontage, and a young maid answered the door. Stephen asked her what year it was, upon which she tried to slam the door in his face. But Stephen barged his way into the hall and the maid screamed to an elderly-looking man who the time-traveller assumed to be the butler. Stephen evaded the servant's attempt to grab him and ran up a flight of stairs. He opened a door that led to a luxurious room where a grey-haired man was sleeping in a high-backed chair in front of a coal fire. Stephen grabbed a newspaper from a table. It was an 1892 copy of *The Times*. He ran with the broadsheet down the stairs, bumping into the old butler, and knocking him over. Out in the street, a caped policeman gave chase, and brought him down with a rugby-style tackle.

Stephen Doherty was arrested by Constable Morrow and marched with his arm up his back to Lark Lane Police Station, where the hippie's appearance, especially his long hair, was mocked by an inspector who questioned his gender. The enlightened man from 1967 told the mundane men from 1892 that he was a time-traveller, and, unable to grasp the concept, they locked him up in the Lark Lane Bridewell. A bemused young police constable, together with an Inspector McKeand, searched Doherty and seemed fascinated by his few possessions; his psychedelic-patterned lighter, a packet of cigarettes, a ten-shilling note and a 1962 Omega wristwatch. McKeand compared the time on his fob watch to the time on the comparatively slim wristwatch and smiled. He said Doherty's timepiece was five hours slow. The inspector then grilled the hippie for his address. 'I don't live here,' Doherty explained, and suddenly stated: 'My name is Stephen Doherty. I was born in 1942. I'm from seventy-five years in the future, and I'm going back soon.'

The inspector turned to an older, chubby desk sergeant who was watching the interrogation with a smirk, and said to him, 'Perhaps we should see what Dr Burnham makes of this one?'

'Aye, sir,' the portly sergeant replied. McKeand and Constable Morrow then scrutinised the unfamiliar crowned woman – the unborn Queen Elizabeth II – on the ten-shilling note. 'Who's she?' the young policeman asked Inspector McKeand. 'I haven't a clue, lad,' he admitted. How would the Victorians know about a monarch from the House of Windsor, which was only founded in 1917?

Doherty asked to see the copy of *The Times* he'd taken from the house named Torrisholme on Aigburth Drive, and McKeand asked him what he wanted with the newspaper. 'I just want to show you a trick I can do with it,' was Doherty's reply. The hippie was given the newspaper, and he rolled it up and sat with it clenched in his fist, cross-legged on the floor of the cell. It was time to go. He closed his eyes and recalled 'The Mantra of Letting Go' as taught to him by the Indian mystic Tarak. Thousands of people go missing each year, and a sizeable percentage of them literally vanish without a trace. Many of these people have in fact stumbled on to the technique of becoming unstuck from their period by ignoring all physical and mental ties with the present. Tarak claimed that H.G. Wells had a friend who could 'drop out' of the present and go anywhere in time, past or future, and this traveller inspired many of the writer's prophetic works.

After a minute of whispering The Mantra of Letting Go, Stephen heard the irritated inspector promising to cut his 'stinking hair' and scrub him clean with a horse's currycomb. Doherty truly let go, the walls of Lark Lane Bridewell fell away into nothingness, and the time-jaunting hippie found himself cart-wheeling through vast spirals of time and space. He hit a pavement slicked with rain on

Aigburth Drive, close to his original point of departure – outside the house where he lodged. He picked himself up and hammered on the door, and Juliet the landlady answered. She hugged him and took Stephen into the warm parlour. He'd vanished from the attic two hours ago, and Juliet told him how he'd faded away like a ghost before vanishing altogether. She dried the soggy August 1892 edition of *The Times* – and that newspaper would later be sent to me as proof of Doherty's time journeys. Three days after the trip into the past, Doherty travelled into the future, and witnessed the 'Liverpool Spacedocks' and an artificial country.

Stephen Doherty told his fascinated landlady Juliet that he intended to explore the infinite territory of time again on 28 April 1967, only this time he was going into the future, something he'd never tried before. Juliet advised against it, sensing something bad in the offing. She had never loved a younger man, and certainly not the hippie type, but 25-year-old Stephen was the exception. She kissed him, and told him to be careful. 'I could teach you to do this you know? We could both hold hands,' Doherty told her, matter of factly, but the landlady was a simple woman, and was content to live in her own time period. She shook her head and sighed.

Doherty sat cross-legged in the dead centre of the carpet. He began the slow breathing exercises, the visualisation of solipsistic isolation, and then, the key to this form of time travel: the Mantra of Letting Go. We are all anchored here, prisoners of the present because we are concerned with the 'Now', and it shall be so until we die. But Stephen's mind is not like yours and mine, and with each breath and inward recitation of the Mantra he slipped away from the illusionary mental state the unenlightened know as the present. The globe of the earth, with its terrifying vastness, turned below him as it wheeled in a helix around the sun, which was in turn tracing a vast curve as it hurtled through the galaxy. At the normal rate, the Earth beneath your feet spins on its axis at 1,000mph, and speeds in its orbit around the sun at 67,000mph, and the sun is orbiting our galaxy at 490,000mph, so you can imagine the complex helical path the world traces through space.

Stephen Doherty, in his transference into the future, travelled that helix within seconds and found himself in an almost unrecognisable Liverpool of centuries hence. By then, Liverpool was a suburb of Northtown, a linear supercity that had absorbed Manchester, Sheffield, Leeds, York and Hull. The Mersey was covered with the gleaming hexagonal launch complexes of the Space Docks. Cammell Laird, once accustomed to producing airtight hi-tech nuclear-powered submarines, now turned out mammoth spaceships driven by antigravity motors to explore and exploit the high frontiers of space. As Doherty looked on in a daze, he saw the interlocking launch pads, standing in the place of the old river, standing there no doubt like the north sea oil platforms of old, covered with a myriad of strange machines and people, all milling about around in an actinic glare. Ships of all sizes and shapes were taking off and landing.

The twentieth century hippie wandered amongst people unborn to us, and he talked to them, but they brushed him aside and communicated with each other in a strange speeded-up way in an unfamiliar accent. They were speaking the global language invented by a computer decades before. An old drop-out sat at the base of a towering structure resembling a lighthouse. Through him, Doherty learned a lot. The man was over a century old, thanks to a longevity drug. The young of the planet had left the earth now that interstellar space travel had become a reality. Some of the youth had gone to colonise a planet named Utopia – the modern name of the 'terraformed' planet of Venus, once a volcanic hell with a poisonous carbon dioxide atmosphere. Genetically modified plants had long since turned the planet into a verdant paradise owned by a former global software company. In the middle of the Atlantic was Atland, an artificial country made by Japanese marine robots. 'Did the peace movement succeed?' Doherty asked the tramp, who laughed. The vagrant then dropped a bombshell – scientists had actually contacted God a few years back.

The time-slipped beatnik crouched and listened in fascination to the tramp, whose name, he learned, was Morley. A 554,000-tonne emigrant ship, *Windermere*, built by Lairds & Boeing, thundered into a sky speckled with sun-glinting vessels at the speed of sound, leaving the familiar Prandtl–Glauert vapour-cone singularity in its wake, miles above the Irish Sea. There was a startling bright blue flash from the *Windermere*, which was carrying another 5,000 people, most of them teens, all deserting the Earth at an escape velocity of over 25,000mph for the new terraformed paradise of Utopia (formerly Venus), 26 million miles away. A sun-drenched day on Utopia, because of the planet's slow rotation, lasts 243 Earth-days – one of the main reasons why it was the new place to be. It took three days and three hours for Apollo 11 to reach the Moon in 1969, and in 2006, NASA's New Horizons probe to Pluto crossed the same Earth-to-Moon distance in 8 hours and 35 minutes. *Windermere* lifted off from Northtown (formerly Liverpool) to reach Venus within two days. The entire surface of the Northtown launch complex pads, which covered the old unseen Mersey from Seaforth to Dungeon Banks, were milling with the space mariners, loading and unloading cargo and personnel from a highly-varied range of spaceships. With the sonic booms and the incessant hubbub of the people and machines, Stephen Doherty struggled to listen to Morley, but would later regret listening to him at all. Doherty quizzed the tramp about the ideology of this strange age, and received a garbled reply. A helmet lined with electronic sensors had made mind-to-mind communication possible in the mid-twenty-first century – and this artificial telepathy had caused worldwide riots.

Chaos reigned as each person discovered what the other person really thought of him or her, and terrible criminal and obscene secrets and hidden desires were ruthlessly uncovered by the new technology. A network of electronic telepaths, similar to the archaic Internet, spread across the globe and almost destroyed society. POL, the world police, outlawed telepathy and imprisoned anyone using a psi-net helmet. A quasi-religious group called the Altruists defied POL and asserted the moral right to participate in a telepathic community. The Altruists credo was alien to everyone: 'To see the world as others see it, to consider the well-being of others before our own.' The Altruists sect believed the evil past ages of humankind were the result of selfish individuals, out for personal gain, forcing their views on the peace-loving masses. The Merger was the Altruist equivalent of the Christian Mass, with the joining of thousands of minds in the Common Consciousness, where whole communities lost their egos and cares as they empathised with other members. As this cult was giving the materialistic capitalist world a tough time, there was another, unexpected ideological upheaval.

An unimaginably complex supercomputer at the Los Alamos National Laboratory in New Mexico, claimed to have decoded a signal from God. The signal, from an unknown source, contained Electronic Voice Phenomena and complex mathematical formulae, explaining the existence of everything and a warning not to skip batches of formulae – or madness would result. Eighty-one scientists who examined the formulae became insane, forty of them became comatose, and three died. 'A few of them recovered and spread the forbidden knowledge,' said Morley. 'I was one of them. I have never recovered. Ignorance is bliss, folly to be wise.' He smiled, then convulsed. Doherty recoiled in terror. Foam issued from the tramp's mouth. 'Shall ... shall I tell you the Ultimate Answer then?' he said.

'I don't want to hear!' Stephen Doherty clamped his hands over his ears and ran off. He hid in a sanitised alleyway of Northtown and decided to go home and escape from the brinks of Hell.

I have amassed over 130 pages of statements from people who knew Doherty, and while some think he was merely a fantasist, others believe he really had developed a mental form of time travel. I am still researching this man and hope to uncover more about him for a future publication.

MING IN MY EAR

Millicent Murphy – or Milly, as she was known to her friends and family – was a beautiful raven-haired girl of just 18 with smouldering hazel eyes and a beautiful figure, indeed her only flaw was the naivety that is inherent in many young people. They say most girls are about five years psychologically ahead of boys of the same physical age, but Milly was an exception. She was indecisive, woolly-minded, and 'slow on the uptake' as we say in these parts, and male scoundrels would always see her coming. Her mum June worried about her naive daughter, and hated days such as these, when Milly would go to town on her own.

It was a typical Saturday afternoon in the autumn of 1974, and Liverpool's Church Street was chock-a-block with shoppers. As Milly was passing Hepworths she tripped slightly, and so she happened to glance down at the pavement in front of a store called Stylo, and it was there she saw a pair of beautiful green earrings lying in the middle of the pavement. She picked them up, looked about furtively and put them in her purse. She soon forgot about the little find and continued to turn male heads as she visited the many shops of the city centre: Wades, Dolcis, Woolworths, Hardy & Willis, and of course, Lewis's. And then Milly Murphy boarded a grass-green 'one-man bus' on Parker Street to take her home.

That night, Milly's older brother Gerry, who knew about everything (it seemed to Milly anyway), confidently stated that the earrings were vintage jade teardrops. 'Genuine Chinese jade, real silver hoops, worth a few bob, them,' Gerry reckoned, and he told Milly that she should have handed the earrings in at the shop near to where she found them.

Milly tried the earrings on in her room before her dresser. They perfectly complemented her hazel eyes, but she hadn't had them on long when she heard a well-spoken yet foreign-sounding voice in her right ear saying, 'Pretty face, poor fate'.

Milly froze, and her big eyes widened with surprise as she gazed at reflection in the mirror. She looked about her room before opening the door to check whether her brother was playing one of his pranks. No one was there. 'Who is that?' she whispered, and that distinctive voice answered: 'Ming. I will enlighten you.'

There was a long pause, during which Milly could actually see her chest quivering from the effects of her rapidly beating heart. She wanted to flee from the room, but then curiosity got the better of her.

'What did you mean, "pretty face, poor fate"? whoever you are,' she asked, her mouth dry with nerves. The voice in one ear said that people with beautiful faces usually had a poor fate because they tended to attract the worst element – the lustful. 'I want to find a man who loves me even after my looks are gone,' Milly confided in the mystical voice, 'Will I find someone genuine?'

'Ming' answered: 'To be loved is above all bargaining, but love thyself first; self-preservation is the first law of nature. Yourself first, others afterwards. Be patient with love, for all comes to she who waits.' And when Milly asked Ming about her string of failed relationships, he advised: 'Respect yourself and others will too.' Milly knew exactly what Ming meant; she shamefully realised she was too 'easy' towards men; she had lost her virginity at the age of 14. She thought of all her faults and suddenly felt incredibly humbled, but Ming seemed to be reading her mind, empathising with her perhaps. He remarked: 'Better for you to be a diamond with a flaw, Milly, than a pebble without one. You are a good girl, and I will try to steer you back on to the right path.'

And the wise sayings and thought-provoking dialogue of Ming filled Milly's head for some time, until she took the jade earrings off. Only then did she realise they were somehow 'haunted' by the unseen sage. Milly changed from that day, she became enlightened, and everyone became aware of the change as the weeks went by. One day Milly's mother and father had a blazing row, and when Milly came downstairs, her parents were busy blaming each other for starting it, and Milly's father asked his daughter: 'Doesn't she always nag me into having a barney?' Milly shrugged and replied: 'There are three sides to every story; your side, Mum's side ... and the truth.'

Milly's parents were so shocked at the depth of the reply they ceased arguing at once.

Men noticed how Milly now said 'no' to their lecherous propositions and always had a witty answer which always left them lost for words. One day, Milly's close friend Frances visited her and Milly could see straight away that she was near to tears. Frances said her cousin Julie had been spreading horrible gossip about her, and

Milly's inner voice helped her offer some sound advice to comfort Frances. Milly merely relayed the counsel. 'Julie is just envious of you, Frances, and envy eats nothing but its own heart. When someone is jealous of you – as Julie is – they envy something you have. You're beautiful, and she's plain-faced; that's why she never goes out without make-up and the most expensive clothes – she needs those distractions because people would see she has no personality.'

Frances giggled when Milly came out with all this.

'Think of jealousy as a type of admiration in warpaint,' Milly continued.

'I hate gossipers, and Julie's the biggest gossiper in Liverpool,' Frances told her friend.

Milly listened to the wise voice in her ear, and then she told Frances: 'A gossip speaks ill of everyone, and everyone will speak ill of her, for those who chatter with Julie will chatter about Julie.'

By the time Frances left that evening, she felt on top of the world, and thanked Milly for her sound advice. Milly couldn't help a little smile: if you only knew – it's not my advice at all, she thought.

The mysterious earrings inexplicably vanished one day, leaving Milly very sad at the loss of Ming, yet enlightened enough to find herself on a course to enjoy life to the fullest. I hope whoever finds the earrings needs them and benefits from their wisdom.

DAYDREAM NUMBER FIVE

The following scatty story supposedly took place back in that long-gone era of open-mindedness and mind-expansion – the Sixties. It was related to me by an old woman called Ada, who has now sadly passed on. Unfortunately, she left me with insufficient details about the people in the story, and so I can only give a tantalizing account of a discovery that promises so much.

One gloomy autumnal afternoon in the September of 1966, two cleaners – Ada and Monica – were at work with elbow grease and

Mansion Polish at a house on Rodney Street. Ada was singing *You Don't Have to Say You Love Me* as she buffed Dr Somerset's antique George III Rosewood tea caddy, and just beyond the doorway, in the oak-panelled hallway of the grand old Georgian house, Monica rested against the newel post at the bottom of the stairs, gasping for a Woodbine and gazing dreamily into space. The mellow saffron luminance of the fading September sun filtering through the grey clouds on high came through the fanlight over the front door, bathing the hallway's panelling with a dull golden light. Certain ambient lighting conditions like this, coupled with a rare atmospheric mood, have been known to invoke peak experiences and strange revelations in the apple of the mind's eye. I once heard of a fifty-something woman, found by her son standing stock-still like a statue at her maisonette window with a look of horror on her face after she had seen lightning strike the Anglican Cathedral. In that millisecond flash, the woman said she had beheld 'the Crack of Doom' – a horrifying vision of how the world would end, but she would burst into tears whenever she tried to tell the curious just what she had seen and she was eventually referred for treatment at a psychiatric hospital.

But back to the house on Rodney Street; this change in Monica's mind wasn't as dramatic as the woman who had seen the End of the World in the lightning flash. The cleaner was always prone to lapse into a reverie, and this was the fifth daydream of that humdrum day. She leaned slightly against the newel post at the foot of the dark, green-carpeted stairway, and her eyes drifted towards an old painting of a country cottage – when something astonishing took place. The leaves on the trees in the painting began to tremble as if stirred by a breeze, and a wisp of blue smoke unfroze from the top of the cottage chimney and swirled skywards. A little black and white cockerspaniel came alive in the painting and ran barking down the path towards Monica, who watched in disbelief as the hallway walls lost their solidity and began to evaporate. All signs of autumn were gone and she found herself immersed in the painting's summer landscape. Still echoing in the distance was Ada's singing, but the Dusty Springfield song was fading fast, until only the barking of the dog and musical background noise of birdsong remained. Monica recalled that the cottage was named Chestnut – her beloved home! It was all coming back now! And the dog was hers – it was little Bessy. And then *he* appeared – the only man Monica had ever loved; he came out of the cottage and stood on the doorstep. 'Where have you been?' he asked, and Monica was about to run to him when she felt a hand at her elbow.

She found herself back in the hallway with a concerned Ada tugging at her arm. 'Monica? Are you alright, chick?' she asked.

At this point, Dr Somerset came out of his surgery and asked what the matter was, and a confused Monica found herself telling him what had happened. She expected him to laugh at the account, but he just looked into her tearful eyes, squeezed her hand, and asked Ada to put the kettle on. Over a cup of tea in the surgery, he asked Monica if she minded him telling a colleague about the strange incident. 'He's a psychiatrist and a hypnotist,' said Somerset.

'Oh no ta, I'm not going tappy, I don't wanna see him,' said Monica.

'No, Monica,' said Somerset, and in a sincere apologetic tone he continued: 'no one is saying you have any condition, but I implore you to see my friend, Dr Playfair. He's looked for so long just to find someone with your talent. Please come with me.'

'Oh, I don't know.' Monica was naturally concerned at the doctor's motives. 'What talent have I got, anyway?'

'Come on, Dr Playfair will explain everything.' Somerset took her to the cloakroom to get the cleaner her coat and took her out of the house, much to the bafflement of poor Ada, who now had to continue her cleaning alone and understaffed.

Monica Hawkins was brought to the rooms of psychiatrist William Playfair, just nine doors down Rodney Street from the surgery of Dr Somerset. When I recently looked at a photograph of Playfair, I was struck by his strong facial resemblance to the late actor Edward Woodward, and from Monica's accounts the psychiatrist shared the same pragmatic, no-nonsense attitude as the thespian. Playfair showed her a Rorschach ink-blot shape and asked her what she could see in it. 'I can see a spadger ...' the cleaner began.

'What on earth is a spadger?' Playfair wanted to know, and Monica explained it was a sparrow.

Playfair encouraged her to go over the strange episode regarding the 'vision' when she had looked into the animated painting, and after Monica's account, he asked her if anything similar had happened before. Monica said the flowers on her bedroom wallpaper had swayed from side to side to strange carnivalesque music when she had scarlet fever as a child.

'But nothing remotely like the incident you experienced today at Dr Somerset's?' Playfair queried, hands clasped, and elbows resting on the green leatherette surface of a huge oaken desk cluttered with books, notes and bottles of ink. Monica slowly shook her head, but then paused and said: 'Well, sometimes I can read people. It's odd.'

'Read people?' Playfair was suddenly all ears. He stood up, in front of the wall decked with a hanging Amritsar carpet, and dressed in a black jacket and black poloneck sweater, he looked stark against the Indian rug's symphony of colour. He folded his arms and asked the cleaner: 'Tell me, Monica, can you read *me*?'

'I've had enough of this lark now, love,' Monica decided, and got up from the chair. 'I've got cleaning to do.' But Playfair begged her to stay, and said he believed she was a 'sensitive' – someone with amazing powers of empathy who could tune in to people, things, photographs, paintings even, to obtain hidden information. Playfair explained how the painting of the cottage hanging in Somerset's hallway had been executed in the 1880s by a relative of his – the wife of the farmer who had lived in that cottage – which was known as The Chesnut. 'That cottage still stands in Lunt, and you somehow tuned into the Victorian lady who painted it,' Playfair told her, but she wasn't having any of it and reached for the doorknob, but the psychiatrist pressed his hand firmly against the door. 'Please work with me,' he said, with a beseeching look in his eyes. Monica could read Playfair, and knew the look was not genuine, but she was curious; what *did* he want her to do?

Reluctantly she turned and went to sit down, and Playfair returned to his desk. 'I have studied sensitives for many years, and I have found that they work best when they are relaxed. You said yourself that you were daydreaming in a relaxed state when you picked up the information from the painting.'

Monica conceded this was true by nodding once.

Playfair scratched his eyebrow, and said: 'I have a very mild anodyne sedative – and I assure you, it's absolutely harmless in its effects – and it will put you in a relaxed state immediately.'

Monica shook her head sternly, but Playfair said he'd pay her a hundred pounds for this experiment; a lot of money in 1966, and Monica had pressing debts. The 'sedative' was liquid ether mixed with lime cordial, and Monica quickly found herself in-between the world of waking and dreaming after sipping the drink. The monochrome photograph Playfair showed her was that of a mutilated body on a bed – a victim of Jack the Ripper.

'You did that!' Monica told Playfair.

Monica tried to get up from the chair but the whole room began to sway from the effects of the ether she had imbibed. William Playfair came around the desk, reaching out in a non-threatening gesture, with one hand. 'You're Jack the Ripper,' Monica repeated, her eyes bulging, and as she backed away her legs gave way from under her. Before she could hit the carpet, Playfair had caught her with amazing reflexes.

'Get away from me, you murdering bastard!' she cried, but Playfair interposed with a weak smile on his face.

'I am not the Ripper, Monica,' he said, and carried the cleaner to his patients' couch. 'Monica, listen!' he gazed into her eyes with a solemn look. 'That was all in a past incarnation, and I regret what I did to those women, but I am trying to understand why I did what I did. You might have done something terrible in your previous life as well you know?'

Monica returned a look of non-comprehension. How could she be expected to know about reincarnation and the countless lives of the human soul?

'I give you my word, Monica, that I am not the monster I was in a previous life. As a psychiatrist I want to understand why I carried out those heinous crimes, and that's where you come in.' Playfair stood up, and then went to sit at his desk, where he hid his face behind splayed fingers.

Monica sat up and suddenly found herself sympathising with him now for some reason.

She asked what he meant; the things about previous lives, and for the next half hour the psychiatrist explained how the souls of most people return from death to a brand new body and live a life all over again, usually with the memories of the previous life erased. 'And how do I come into all this?' Monica asked, 'Why do you need me?'

'You're a sensitive,' William answered, 'and you can read what isn't even noticed by most people. I want you to look at a very old painting ... a painting which contains hidden information ... that will allow me ... and you too if you'd like ... to travel through time.'

Playfair opened the wide middle drawer in the desk and took out a familiar painting : the Mona Lisa – Leonardo da Vinci's most famous portrait of a Florentine nobleman's wife. Monica gazed at the detailed print of the painting, and slowly realised what da Vinci was trying to convey in the geometric patterns that formed the background to the most famous lady in the world; the S-curve of the road, the series of arched bridges and even the seemingly random crags. 'He was from the future,' Monica told an enthralled-looking Playfair, 'a time-traveller. Get me paper and a pencil and I will draw the engine he used for his time machine.'

'Oh, yes!' Playfair said with delight, and he slapped a pad and biro down by Monica, then watched the gifted cleaner's long fingers effortlessly sketch in the trademark style as Leonardo. She explained how the engine was to be activated and controlled using high voltages, then slumped forwards as the ether wore off. When Monica awoke on the couch, Playfair told her: 'Monica, I am going to build a time machine in the next room and I will go back and psychoanalyse Jack the Ripper, then perhaps dine on the *Titanic*. Would you be prepared to explore the corridors of time with me?'

'Oh, alright, love,' said Monica. 'And can we see those pyramids bein' built?'

'Absolutely!' Playfair promised, and kissed Monica's knuckle.

Monica excitedly told Ada about the time machine that Playfair was building, but Ada thought her friend was losing her marbles. Ada also noticed a twinkle in the cleaner's eye which suggested she had a bit of a thing for the doctor. Not long afterwards, Monica moved out of her little flat in north Liverpool, and she, and Dr Playfair, were allegedly seen no more. Did they take that trip in a time machine or just take a trip on each other's new-found love? We'll probably never know.

TRUTH WINE

The following true story took place in the mid-1970s. A popinjay of immense vanity named Burt lived on his looks and ruthlessly honed fake sincerity, and wherever a woman was to be found, be it in a club or a library, Burt would 'soft-soap' her with flattery and well-rehearsed lines of the most elaborate sweet talk. He really had mastered the art of sycophancy. He was undoubtedly good-looking, but the face is no index of the heart, and every romantic remark, every love-letter and glint of the eye was thoroughly and coldly premeditated. Even men seemed to find Burt a decent and likeable friend; a confidant you could unload any confession to – even though Burt was 40-faced and took great delight in destroying people's reputations behind their backs. His mask of decency slipped a few times. Seven girlfriends back, poor Jo was out buying him a birthday present one afternoon and caught him passionately kissing a middle-aged woman outside the Globe pub on Cases Street. Jo's parting warning words to the scoundrel were: 'You'll get your come-uppance! I promise you that!'

Burt thought he knew women and therefore believed he would never get this 'come-uppance'; he convinced himself that there was a system to win any woman over and he was well-versed in this philandering method – or so he thought. He decided to teach himself a bit about the mind to improve his womanising ways, and so he visited Parry's bookshop on Bold Street, where he browsed through a copy of *Psychology Made Simple*. And there at the bookshop he spotted Selena Bray, stacking the shelves. She was absolutely beautiful and her voice reminded him of Audrey Hepburn. Perhaps she was the one to actually keep as a wife; he could still carry out his heartbreaking trade of course, but she could become a fixed point in his life and provide him with some home comforts.

He chatted 25-year-old Selena up, took her to an expensive restaurant where the striking bookshop employee insisted on paying for everything. And to top it all, a certain detective named Roberts, who had long hated Burt because he was a pitiless gigolo, sat on the very next table with his wife. Oh, how envious the copper would be! Selena ordered a bottle of 'vin la vérité' and Burt found this unfamiliarly-titled purple wine sweet but delicious.

'What do you really see in me?' Selena asked with smiling eyes.

Burt clenched his teeth, because he found himself wanting to give a honest reply. He just had to speak, even though he tried desperately not to. 'Because you have a lovely body and you're gullible,' he rasped.

Selena was not at all insulted, but smiled and raised her eyebrows.

Inspector Roberts thinned his eyes in disbelief as he listened in from the neighbouring table.

'I bet you tell all the girls that ...' Selena murmured, and Burt shook his head with a confused look.

'No, I lie to them,' he replied, and tried to clamp his hand over his lips. He desperately wanted to shut up but couldn't. He answered every question posed by Selena with clinical honesty, and the truths he revealed were disgusting and disgraceful. They also shocked Inspector Roberts, because Burt revealed he'd once had an affair with Mrs Roberts! Mrs Roberts blushed heavily when this truth came out, and she looked light-headed as if she was about to faint.

Every dark secret entrusted to Burt – some from hardened criminals – came out of his blabbering mouth thanks to that wine, and he was promptly arrested by the inspector.

Selena feigned shock as the arrest was made, and she put her hand to her mouth and hurried sobbing into the ladies. Mr Roberts never saw her come out of that toilet. A beautiful mature lady did come out though, and passing Burt she intoned: 'You got your comeuppance, eh?' Burt recognised the Audrey Hepburn voice; it was Selena, but who would believe him? Betrayed, Jo's grandmother – a practising witch of the Childwall Coven – relished the revenge.

A few years after this incident, when Burt came out of jail, he visited the bookshop on Bold Street and was told by the employees that they could recall no one working at Parry's with the name Selena. And at the expensive restaurant where Burt had been stricken with that strange condition whereby he found himself compelled to tell the truth, he scanned the wine lists and saw that there was no wine called vin la vérité – French, of course, for Wine of Truth.

Ask Mr Aries

The following eerie story was told to me many years ago by antiques expert Brian Kettering, a very knowledgeable man who had tried out a number of interesting jobs in his younger days, one of which was private detective. The year was 1966, and in the summer of that year, Brian, aged 26, had a small office on Liverpool's Renshaw Street, just a few doors away from the office of *Mersey Beat* newspaper, at number 81a. Brian rarely had any exciting cases to investigate, and upon this sunny afternoon, when he would soon find himself embroiled in a very strange case, he was concerned with tracing a lost pedigree dog that had been stolen from a house in south Liverpool. As Brian's client, a woman in her late sixties, left the office, a friend called at the Renshaw Street premises. The caller was 25-year-old James Malt, and he had known Brian since his childhood days, and now, after taking a week's holiday from his job with a plumbing firm, he had decided to call upon him to see if his old friend fancied going for a lunchtime drink.

Brian was glad to see Jim, as he called Malt, not least because he wanted an excuse to leave the warm stuffy office for a break. Jim suggested the Vines pub, and when they walked towards Lime Street's grandest watering hole, Brian pointed to the huge clock hanging from the side of the pub and told his friend that it had been made by the same firm that had built Big Ben down in Westminster. The bit of trivia went over Jim Malt's head, because Jim had just noticed a crowd at the Copperas Hill entrance to the Vines, and when he and Brian reached the pub, they saw that the crowd had formed because a very famous comedian was inside. According to Brian, Tony Hancock, the greatest radio and television star of his era, had been based at the Adelphi Hotel during his summer show at Blackpool, and had decided one day to go across the road from the hotel to the Vines.

Unknown to most people at the time, Tony had a serious interest in philosophy and mysticism, and as he drank at the Vines, he happened to look up and notice the weird moulding of a face that was the personification of the Devil, gazing down at him from the ceiling of the bar. Tony was unnerved yet fascinated by the horned plaster face with its piercing red eyes, and one of the drinkers present – a man in his seventies – said the demonic face was nicknamed Mr Aries, and was thought to represent the Ram as part of the other Zodiac mouldings set on the pub's ceiling. Bob Kettering and Jim Malt stayed at the pub for almost an hour, and were lucky enough to obtain Tony Hancock's autograph before a policeman arrived to control the crowds. Tony Hancock was a renowned heavy drinker, and at one point as he sat in the bar, drinking shorts, the old man sitting at the star's table suddenly said, 'Mr Aries up there can tell you things about yourself that you didn't know if you look at his red eyes long enough.'

Hancock gave a slight sneer and deliberately gazed up at the uncanny face as laughter rippled through the crowd of fans. But then a few minutes later, the most famous and most-loved comedian in the country looked up at Mr Aries – and this time a look of absolute horror darkened his face. His trademark heavy-lidded expressive blue eyes widened. There were a few sniggers, but then Brian

Kettering realised that 'the lad himself' as Hancock was humourously nicknamed, was not clowning about on this occasion. Hancock let out a cry, as if he'd had some ghastly vision. At this point, a policeman pushed Brian and Jim out the door and the two young men walked off into the July sunshine, baffled as to what the entertainer had seen.

Of course, Hancock had a turbulent relationship with drink, and was also known as a pill-popper. He took a rainbow of sedative pills for his depression and his drinking spiralled out of control as he found himself plagued with self-doubt about his talent as a top-earning comedian. He needn't have worried about his talent, because Hancock was a natural-born comedian, but worry he did, and upon searching for a way to re-invent himself, he hastily got rid of his popular co-star on *Hancock's Half-Hour*, Sid James, and he then sacked his scriptwriters Galton and Simpson. He tried to become an international star like his idol Chaplin, but found that his brand of humour did not travel well. Too many drinks and pills soon put paid to his ailing career, and after an attempt to make the grade in Australia, he conceded that his heavy drinking and pill-taking were making it almost impossible to learn his lines.

Years before this sorry state of affairs, the comedic genius Spike Milligan had remarked how Tony Hancock had been a difficult man to work with, and how he had got rid of everyone in his life, adding prophetically that it was only a matter of time before he got rid of himself.

On the morning of Monday, 24 June 1968, the body of Tony Hancock, aged 44, was found in his room in his Bellevue Hill flat in Sydney. The comedian had died from a sizeable overdose of amylobarbitone tablets washed down by a half-size $1.67 bottle of vodka. Those who discovered Tony's body were greeted with a macabre sight. He was gazing at the ceiling with his eyes wide open, and the cigarette in his left hand had burned down to his fingers. In his other hand, Tony held the ballpoint pen with which he had written several suicide notes, and they lay near his body. They had been written on the backs of two pages of a script Tony had been trying unsuccessfully to learn.

The first note stated that the act of suicide was 'quite rational' and one line instructed: 'Please give my love to my mother, but there was nothing left to do. Things seemed to go too wrong too many times.'

In the second suicide note, Tony expressed his apologies to his mother for his suicide, but stated that: 'the soul is indestructible' in some attempt at reassurance. The note's last four lines then become unintelligible at the point at which the comedian must have found himself sinking into unconsciousness.

When Brian Kettering heard of Hancock's untimely death on a television news programme, he was naturally shocked and saddened like many other fans of the legendary comedian, but then he recalled that day when Tony Hancock had looked up at 'Mr Aries' in the Vines, and he wondered if the comedian had foreseen his own grim future that afternoon. Out of sheer macabre curiosity, Brian decided that in the near future he would go and look at that creepy horned head with the red eyes on the pub ceiling.

On the Thursday evening of 31 October – at Halloween, of all times – he visited the pub with his friend Jim, and the two of them sat talking about Hancock's suicide and what a tragic waste of talent it was. The two men looked up at Mr Aries as they each enjoyed a pint of mild, but then Jim Malt suddenly became fixated with the scarlet eyes of the Pan-like face, and his jaw dropped. Brian's eyes had been wandering over a plaster frieze on the wall, but then he suddenly noticed the spellbound face of his chum and asked him if he was alright. Getting no reply, Brian waved his palm to and fro in front of Jim's eyes. Jim snapped out of the spell and then looked at Brian with an expression of intense worry.

'What is it Jim?' Brian asked, and he seized his friend by the arm and shook him.

'I saw some sort of vision,' Jim replied, with tears welling in his eyes, 'and it was horrible.' He told Brian he had foreseen himself as drunken brute, years into the future, and he was beating his wife – a blonde woman he had never even seen before. He then saw himself driving a car whilst drunk, and that car mowed down a little girl.

Jim was so affected by the vision, he became teetotal, and many years later he met and married a blonde woman called Moira, and she looked exactly like the woman he had seen in that awful glimpse of what must have been a 'possible' future for him that Halloween in 1968.

The carvings and mouldings that form the Zodiac on the ceiling of the bar of the Vines were designed by Walter W. Thomas (who, incidentally also designed the interior of the Philharmonic pub), back in 1907. Thomas had a fascination with gargoyles and also the subject of the occult, and I wonder what inspired his designs for the astrological features of his work, which is of course, still on show in the Vines, if you care to inspect it ...

WALTON WITCHERY

I'm sure most of the people of Walton, or Waltonians as they should be addressed correctly, will know of the Old Rectory, a stone and slate Grade II listed building in Walton Village that is well over 200 years old, and also haunted, by repute, though this fact has nothing much to do with the story I am about to tell you, but it's worth mentioning in passing because little publicity is ever given to the building's resident ghost. A mysterious cloaked figure in black haunts the Old Rectory, and he has been seen by scores of people over the decades, roaming the stairways and the rooms which used to be servants' quarters. When renovations were ongoing at the Rectory some years ago, workmen refused to work once twilight descended because they experienced so many strange goings-on. Specialist lighting equipment consisting of extra-bright halogen lamps had to be brought in at one point of the renovation in the hope that the actinic light would keep the supernatural forces at bay.

In the mid-1980s a fire broke out in the basement of the Old Rectory one morning around dawn, and the fire brigade were soon upon the scene to tackle the blaze. After the fire was brought under control, a fireman happened to glance out through an upstairs window, and was rather intrigued and a little alarmed to see a man in black, wearing a cloak, standing beside the fire engine parked in the grounds below. The man in black seemed fascinated by the fire engine and kept watching all of the activity that morning until he suddenly vanished.

For years there have been rumours that the man in black comes up from the basement of the Old Rectory from an undiscovered system of tunnels that runs beneath the streets of Walton Village and beyond. Workmen laying pipes in the area near the Old rectory in the 1930s claimed that they had found a tunnel which ran to Walton Church. Some of the older people in the area recalled the sounds of voices coming from a grid near Walton Church in the 1920s, but for some reason, the workmen were told to fill in the entrance to the unknown tunnel, and today, no one is any the wiser as to the purpose of the secret network beneath Walton.

Just a stone's throw from the Old Rectory, there was a beautiful old detached house for sale in the early 1970s, but everyone who tried to live in it ended up moving out within weeks, and sometimes just days, because it was said to be extremely haunted.

In the late summer of 1971 the Standish family bought the house for about £70,000 and each family member settled into the residence, which dated back to early Victorian times. The youngest member of the family, nine-year-old Judy Standish, felt there was something almost magical yet creepy about the back garden of the house, which was disproportionately huge compared to the front garden. Judy noticed a slight mound in the middle of the back garden, and walked around it trying to guage its size. It was, in her estimation, about 15 feet in diameter, but the girl's parents and older brothers took no notice as Judy tried to describe the small knoll. Judy's bedroom looked out on to the back garden, and on the third night at the new house, just after midnight, when she was supposed to be tucked up in bed and sound asleep, she was leaning on the windowsill, dreamily gazing up at the full moon and musing upon the circular interference effects and moiré patterns the lunar orb created through the finely-woven diaphanous net curtain, when something caught her eye below.

An abnormally tall man stood in the middle of the garden – upon that small mound, and he was looking directly up at her. Whoever he was, he was just a silhouette in the moonlight, but Judy just knew – just sensed with a shudder – that he could see her peeking through the net curtains at him, and she backed away from the window and ran into her brother Russell's room to tell him about the weird tall trespasser. Russell, who had just turned 13, had just nodded off and was rather grumpy when Judy awakened him with a frantic shaking of his shoulder. She told him about the stark shadowy figure, and badgered Russell until he threw back the covers with a grunt and stormed from the bed to see what she was talking about. There was no one in the garden when he looked out of the window and he told Judy she was imagining things. Judy insisted she was not seeing things but Russell went back to bed, leaving his sister alone and nervous in the bedroom. She called after her brother with a whimper in her voice, but he slammed the door of his room hard behind him.

Judy got back into bed but kept looking at the window, expecting the silhouetted head of the man she had seen earlier to appear at any minute through the panes, even though she was on the first floor of her house. She silently said her prayers and dozed off before she could reach 'Amen'. A noise woke her. She felt so strange as she got out of bed with a peculiar numbness in her legs and a lack of feeling in all her limbs. She went to the window, lifted the lacey white curtains, and looked out. The moon was still illuminating the garden with its silvery-grey radiance. Judy opened the window, and looked down.

He was standing among the border of flowers, 20 feet below, and his ghastly pale face was tilted up at her. Judy froze. His eyes were just two black almonds. Judy tried but could not move an inch to get away from that window, nor could she turn her face away. It felt as if her head was locked in place so she was forced to look at him. He lifted his leg and put the sole of his right foot against the wall.

Why is he doing that? she wondered. And then he began to walk up the wall towards her. She tried to scream but the intended cry couldn't escape her throat.

Meanwhile, the elongated man in black bolted up the wall ...

... then Judy woke up with a start in bed. She opened her eyes and heard her heart thrumming blood inside her chest. The full moon had risen a little higher. She slowly turned to look at the bedside clock and found it was nearly one in the morning. What a horrible dream, she thought, and the mood of dread spilled over from the nightmare into her waking life, making her too scared to even go to the toilet. Judy held out for as long as she could, and when she heard Russell on the landing outside at 1.40am on his way to the toilet, she ran to meet him, startling him. 'Can I go to the toilet first?' she asked, 'I've just had a really bad nightmare.'

'Hurry up then, you nuisance,' said Russell, and waited as Judy dashed to the toilet.

A few nights after this, Judy went up to her bedroom at 9pm, having promised her mother she would not look out of the window or imagine any more bogeymen. She said she would read *Tales After Tea* by Enid Blyton, a favourite of hers and just the type of light reading she needed to dispel all dark and supernatural thoughts.

Judy settled down with three pillows propped up behind her as she read the book by the light of her bedside lamp. After quarter of an hour her mind began to wander, as did her eyes, away from the pages of the Enid Blyton book towards the window. The moon rises later each night, and as of yet it hadn't peeped over the rooftops in the east. Judy fought the urge to satisfy her morbid curiosity and tried to read on. It was impossible. It was as if something was urging her to look out of the window. From the little cupboard in the bedside cabinet, she retrieved a brand new Sylvine drawing pad her grandmother had bought her, and a few felt tip pens, and began to draw a little house, which consisted of the usual rectangle with four squares set in it, and a triangle for a roof. Judy sketched the rectangular chimney stack and its pots, and scribbled a little wiggly line to represent smoke. She then put the drawing book down, delved into the cupboard again, and found an old comic of her brother's that she had borrowed. She flipped through the comic, which happened to be *The Sparky*, then momentarily glanced back at the drawing pad on the bed.

Next to her sketch of the house there was now a childish drawing of the mound – and a matchstick man standing in the middle of it.

Then the girl realised that her curtains were fluttering in the breeze, because the window was now open. Judy calmly got out of bed and left the room. She went downstairs and as she hurried into the living room, her mother, who was watching a late-night film with her husband, let out a weary sigh, 'Oh what is it now, Judy?'

Judy burst into tears and told her mother and father about the uncanny sketch of the mound in the garden and the matchstick man, but they thought that she had done the drawing herself, perhaps just for attention. However, when Mrs Standish took her daughter up to the bedroom, she had to think again. One of the felt tip pens was standing up vertically in the middle of the page in the drawing pad which featured Judy's sketch of a house, along with the alleged drawing made by a ghost. The felt tip pen waltzed around the page as mother and daughter looked on in horror, and that pen wrote: GET OUT OF THIS HOUSE OR DIE.

As if that wasn't terrifying enough, a phantom hand suddenly slapped Judy's mother across the face and sent her reeling towards a corner of the room, where she landed on her backside in shock. Judy became hysterical, and unseen hands grabbed at her long hair and began to pull and shove her around the room. Mr Standish heard the commotion coming from Judy's room, and was soon bounding up the stairs two at a time. Judy's three brothers were woken by the screams and they came out on to the landing to see their father arrive at the doorway of Judy's room. Mr Standish screwed his eyes up and cried out in agony as red scratches appeared down his cheek. He raised his hands to protect himself.

'Get out of this house or you'll all die!' screeched a female voice, then Judy and her traumatised mother and badly-shaken father heard running footsteps going towards the window in Judy's room.

The family were so afraid of the terrifying events of that night, they went to stay in a friend's house in Branstree Avenue in Norris Green until Mr Standish could convince a priest to bless their new home. The priest blessed the house and things seemed to be okay for a while, but at the beginning of October, all hell broke loose one night when a cutlery drawer flew open all by itself and knives shot out everywhere, some narrowly missing Mrs Standish, who was preparing supper. An invisible finger wrote the words GET OUT OR DIE on the steamed-up window in the kitchen, and then came the grisly apparition of a headless woman in Russell's room at one in the morning. Russell was woken by the window handle of his room squeaking as it turned by itself. The window then swung open, and he heard footsteps by his bed. Then, in the shadow next to his wardrobe, he noticed a woman dressed in black and dark-brown old-fashioned clothes, holding a basket covered with a gingham cloth.

When this apparition stepped out of the shadows, Russell could see it had no head. The ghost's pale hand lifted and its finger and thumb turned back a corner of the gingham cloth to reveal a severed head with two red sockets for eyes. The mouth of this head screamed so loud, Russell was left with a ringing in his ears as he ran from his bed, urinating as he went, and pulled the doorknob with such force, it came off in his hand – so he was unable to get out of the room. He screamed and ran to the window, intending to jump out, just to get away from the headless horror, but the door flew open as Mr Standish pushed it from the outside. As he came into the room, the headless woman vanished.

The traumatised family couldn't take any more and decided to move out of the house that night, and it is said that they found accommodation for a while in their friend's house in Norris Green before they found a much more normal house, devoid of any supernatural terrors, in Knowsley.

The house in Walton Village was once again unoccupied, and people who had lived in the area around the dwelling were not too surprised at the departure of yet another family. But then in March 1973, a bachelor in his early sixties, Frederick Parr, arrived at the infamous house one morning with a very nervous estate agent for a viewing of the property. The estate agent was very surprised when Parr told him he was aware of the house's paranormal reputation, and that he wanted to buy the property so he could get to the bottom of the haunting. The estate agent certainly didn't try to dissuade Parr from buying the property, which is known as a 'hard-to-let' in the world of real estate.

The house with the over-commodious back garden was sold for £65,000 to Parr, and on the very first night at the house, he heard heavy footsteps in the attic as he lay in bed, followed by thumps on the walls, then the sounds of clinking chains being dragged across the ceiling filled the bedroom. 'Is that the best you can do?' he shouted, and the racket died down. Parr took the notebook from his bedside cabinet and began to jot down the time of the 'poltergeist outbreak' with a pencil. There was no further supernatural activity that night, but Mr Parr spent the remainder of that night practically sleeping like a fox with one eye open.

On the following day, along with the usual manila envelopes containing bills, on the doormat was a vanilla-coloured envelope that had been posted in person by the sender, a Miss Eleanor Ival, the secretary of the Walton Village History Society, according to the printed letterhead on the sheet of quality stationery. It was an invitation to a tea party at a local house, and Miss Ival explained that Mr Parr had been invited because his house was of great historical significance and she thought he would be interested in the talk that would be delivered by local historian Mavis Dunstable, because it included the 'strange history' of Mr Parr's residence.

Parr accepted the invitation, and attended the tea party, which took place a week later. Eleanor Ival was a beautiful red-haired lady, possibly in her thirties, with a rather pallid complexion. Her gentle hand shook Parr's coarse gripping hand, and she seated him at a long table at the end of a spacious parlour where some twelve women were assembled. Frederick Parr was the only man in attendance. Tea was served with cakes of all varieties, all of them home baked, according to Miss Ival, and then Mavis Dunstable, a tall slim lady of about 40 with long straight coal-black hair and penetrating dark brown eyes, stood in front of a fireplace where a white screen had been set up. Mavis nodded to a woman at the end of the table who rose, closed the curtains, and then operated the slide projector as Mavis began her lecture on the history of Walton, and Walton Village in particular.

The slide which depicted the house Parr had purchased appeared, and he studied its image, thrown on to the large screen. It showed the house as it had appeared long ago, in Edwardian times, according to Mavis Dunstable. She gave a potted history about the various people and families who had lived at the house. Mavis talked of tobacconists, greengrocers, bookkeepers, confectioners and bankers who had lived at the address now occupied by Parr, but then she began to show yellowed newspaper cuttings on the screen, taken from local newspapers of long ago, and each cutting mentioned the curse which was said to afflict all those who lived at the house. Over twenty families and eight individual occupants of the house had been forced to leave by the violent ghosts, Mavis claimed, and then began to rattle off some of the most spine chilling ghost stories Parr had ever heard, and at the epicentre of these tales of terror was his very own house.

At the end of the talk, the women applauded, and so did Parr, and over the last cups of tea and cake at the gathering, Miss Ival asked him if he had ever experienced anything remotely supernatural since he had moved in. Parr said he had heard thumps, footsteps and the sound of chains being dragged and shaken in the attic. 'Oh, how terrible,' said Miss Ival, 'were you scared Mr Parr?'

'Not really,' was Parr's surprising reply. 'It struck me as pretty mediocre, actually.'

'Mediocre?' Miss Ival seemed perplexed by Parr's complacency.

Parr nodded after taking a bite of sandwich cake. 'Yes, it was a rather run-of-the-mill haunting really. What do ghosts hope to achieve by rattling chains and banging on walls?'

That night, at 11pm, Parr retired to his bedroom with a transistor radio, a cup of tea, and a notebook and pencil in which to record any further paranormal goings-on, should they occur. A few times he dozed off with the radio still on. At 2.20am, the bedroom window began to rattle violently, and then it slid upwards as if opened by invisible hands. The curtains then parted, and a shrieking wind blasted into the room. Parr's shoes, which had been left at the side of the bed, were lifted up into the air and began to clobber him on his head and arms. Then the alarm clock was sucked aloft, along with the half-drunk cup of tea and its saucer, the pencil and notebook. And then the radio floated into the air, and its tuning knob must have been turned by the invisible mischief-maker, because there was a medley of orchestral music, foreign voices and static from the radio as it sailed up into the air. Every object in the bedroom seemed to be hanging in mid-air as if the entire house was in free-fall. Then something began to shake the bed.

'Stop this, in the name of God! Stop it!' Parr shouted, and then he suddenly held out his palm towards the thing at the bottom of the bed which was shaking the mattress. On each of his palms he had drawn circles with strange crosses within them which resembled the 'double cross' of Lorraine; symbols which were used to counteract witchcraft by the old occultists.

Parr began to recite the words of an ancient grimoire in Latin, and as he did so, screams rent the air.

At the bottom of the bed, clad in a long black flowing robe, there appeared a very familiar woman: none other than Eleanor Ival!

She screamed as she saw the symbols on Parr's outstretched palms, and as he began to repeat the mystical words of the grimoire, Ival squeezed her eyes shut, then dived through the open window, but instead of arcing downwards, she flew upwards and out through the window.

The radio, cup of tea, notebook, pencil and shoes clattered to the floor and on to the bed as the weird phenomena came to an abrupt end. Frederick Parr, occultist and modern-day witchfinder had confirmed his suspicions about the house. He had researched its history and discovered that the ground in the back garden had long been regarded as a sacred site where witches held their Sabbaths. Parr had known all the time that the so-called historical society he had had his tea and cake with was actually a local coven of witches, which explained the absence of any men. Parr attempted to confront Miss Ival at the building where she was supposedly a secretary for the historical society, but discovered that the house had lain empty for a few months, and had evidently been cleaned up by the coven members to stage their mock tea party event. Parr persisted in trying to contact Miss Ival, but found it impossible, for she seemed to disappear, along with the other 'local historian' Mavis Dunstable.

Parr was convinced that there was something beneath that mound in the back garden, and planned to make excavations with a few friends – but just before the excavations were to get underway, Frederick Parr suffered a massive heart attack, and his body was found in the garden, face down, with his limbs in what was described as 'an unnatural posture'. It was believed that he had died in the house, but had been dragged outside after his death and placed on the mound. On the night of Parr's unfortunate demise, it is said that the witches danced in a circle on the moonlit mound.

If, from what I have told you, you work out where this mound is, stay well away from it. I hear that one of the most powerful witches in our neck of the woods now lives in the house in which Frederick Parr lived – and died.

A Strange Walton Hall Avenue Haunting

Regular readers of my books will know that many stories come my way which are particularly baffling and defy logical explanation. What follows is just one of these accounts.

Early in 2008 at a Victorian terraced house at the Queens Drive end of Walton Hall Avenue, a couple in their thirties, Mike and Laura, began stripping the walls of the spare room at their home and repainting them buttermilk, a colour that Mike despised, but he knew it was pointless to argue with Laura once she had made her mind up. The window in the spare room had been used by Mike to store all of his old books, comics, annuals and various items of junk which dated back to his teens, and now all of it had to be moved up into the loft. Laura wanted to turn the room into a guest bedroom, a place where her mother and various friends could stay during visits, but Mike was afraid it would only encourage his mother-in-law, Sheila – a woman he just could not get on with – to outstay her welcome for an even longer and more unbearable period of time. The couple had lived at the terraced house for almost ten years, and had talked about moving to Ormskirk now and then. They were both from Walton, but fancied retiring to the rural parts of Ormskirk one day, if only Mike could get a better-paid job.

Mike sprayed lukewarm water on to the dreadful woodchip wallpaper put up by the previous occupants, then vigorously slid the wallpaper scraper up and down. There were two other layers of older wallpaper beneath the woodchip. The wintry daylight from the window which looked on to Walton Hall Park was steadily dying, so Mike switched on the light and continued his work. He was about to shout Laura to ask what she was doing (for she had promised to help him) but then he could smell her frying something downstairs and realised she had sneaked off to cook the tea.

And then the odd discovery was made. A section of bare wall measuring about four feet by two feet was uncovered, and it looked as if someone had painted something on to it. fascinated by the partially revealed image, Mike carefully scraped away more and more layers of the old wallpaper until a peculiar painting was revealed which depicted a tall archway with a corridor leading from it into the distance. The perspective was amazing, and Mike felt as if he could just step into the painting and walk down the long corridor. It looked almost three-dimensional. Mike tried to call up Laura to see the strange work of art but she shouted back, 'I'll come up later, I'm cooking!'

By the time Laura came up to the room, Mike had uncovered the rest of the bizarre out-of-place mural. It showed that the archway was surrounded by gothic designs and black marble gargoyles. Laura swore, then gasped: 'What the ... what is that?'

'That's got to date back to the Edwardian or Victorian days,' Mike opined, his face flushed from all the energetic scraping and spraying.

'It's got to go, though,' said Laura emphatically.

'Are you round the bloomin' bend?' said Mike recoiling in disbeleif, 'That's probably worth a few bob, it's art, Laura!'

'Well can't you peel it off or take it off the wall somehow?' Laura asked, and moved a bit closer to inspect the weird images of the gargoyles. She sensed the massive eight-foot-square painting had an evil aura, and didn't want to get too close.

'It's painted on the bare plaster,' Mike told her with a vague smile of condescension, 'you can't peel it off.'

'Well it's not staying,' Laura crossed her arms and looked at the wall sternly. 'This is my new guest bedroom.'

'You're unbelievable,' said Mike turning his back on her. 'Talk about a Philistine.'

Laura flounced downstairs to have a sulk.

Mike went out of the room, looked over the banister, and then took out his mobile phone and called his friend Pete Hammond, who lived just a mile away. Pete knew everything about antiques, and presumably old murals as well. When Pete heard about the painting of the arch, he said it sounded like an example of what is known as a trompe-l'oeuil.

'I knew you'd have an idea what it was,' Mike told him, and asked just what a trompe-l'oeuil was.

'It's French for deceive the eye,' Pete Hammond replied, 'and its an art technique where the painter skilfully creates a very realistic image which looks three-dimensional. Like the old backdrops you see in some stage plays to create an illusion of depth. Take a photo of it, mate, and send it over.'

Mike took a picture of the trompe-l'oeuil on his phone and sent it to Pete. A minute later, Pete texted Mike to say he'd be right over.

Laura was not keen on Pete Hammond for some reason, so Mike didn't tell her he was coming over, and Laura only realised when she saw Pete pulling up outside in his car.

'Why's he here?' Laura shot a suspicious look at Mike, who was already leaving the living room to open the door to Pete.

Pete smiled as he entered the house and had just got as far as the vestibule doorway when Laura said to him, 'We're busy decorating; why didn't you phone first?'

Pete realised his meek friend had not told his partner about the visit, and covered for Mike by saying, 'Sorry, I was just passing.'

But Laura quickly cottoned on to the truth, because Pete went straight upstairs with Mike to see the mural – as if he already knew what had been found. Pete seemed to be in awe of the trompe-l'oeuil, and took pictures of it on his own phone. He examined the mural closely, running his fingertips over it. 'You should find out who lived here in the 1900s,' Pete suggested, crouching as he examined the intricate patterns on one of the pillars to the left of the arch. 'It's a very old painting, oils, but there's a sheen on it, a glaze of some sort. What's it supposed to be? Just ornamental perhaps.'

Pete Hammond's further comments on the mural were cut short by Laura, who came into the room with great urgency in her voice. 'Mike, Mum's coming down in a minute. There's been an incident. She's in a terrible state,' she said, and glanced at the mobile in her hand.

'Oh,' Mike replied, caught unawares by the news.

'So you'd better be getting off soon, Pete, I'm sorry,' said Laura to Pete who was still crouched at the base of the intriguing painting.

As soon as Laura had hurried down the stairs, Pete stood up and in a sombre tone said to Mike, 'You want to start standing up to her, mate,' and then he headed out of the room and went down the stairs. As Pete's car pulled away, Mike said to Laura: 'You don't want any of my mates coming here, do you?'

Laura didn't even look up at him. She looked at the label of the five-litre can of Dulux on the coffee table, then said: 'We're supposed to be decorating, and you know very well once you invite Pete Hammond over he eats us out of house and home and stays here all night.'

'Is your mother really coming over, and has there been an "incident" then?' Mike asked through gritted his teeth, 'Or was that just an excuse to get rid of Pete?'

After a long pause, Laura picked up the remote and lowered the volume on the television. 'Yeah, it was,' she said.

'You're unbelievable.'

Mike left the living room and went back up to strip the other three walls. The plan was to let the walls dry out overnight and then to begin applying the paint, without a primer, as Mike had repeatedly suggested to Laura.

Just after 3am that morning, Mike was startled out of his sleep by

Laura shaking his shoulder. 'What?' he said, his throat hoarse and dry.

'There're funny noises coming from the room,' Laura whispered, and as Mike asked: 'What noises?' she put her finger to her lips and whispered, 'Listen!'

Mike could hear nothing much at first: maybe a police or paramedic siren somewhere in the distance, probably coming from Walton Queens Drive. The siren faded into the stillness. And then he heard a distant voice; someone shouting an unintelligible word. Laura looked at the wall, at the other side of which was the spare room. The voice was definitely coming from that room.

Mike swung out of bed and crept to the door in nothing but his boxer shorts. He looked back at Laura, who had now switched on the bedside lamp. He crept to the room next door, and as soon as he entered, he switched on the old 100-watt tungsten filament bulb, and its yellowish stark light instantly lit up an empty room. A few black plastic bin-liners filled with stripped paper lay against one wall and for some reason, Laura had left her mobile phone on the window ledge.

Then Mike realised there was something moving on the wall – *within* that mural. A figure, just a few inches in length, was coming down the long corridor, getting closer and closer – and whoever it was, they were ranting and screeching something as they waved a sword about. The mural was no longer flat and two-dimensional; it now seemed to have depth, as if a real corridor was leading to the spare room, complete with a madman wielding a sword. The figure was now about five or six inches tall, and he could see that he was wearing a pointed hood and long cloak like a monk's. Mike also noticed flickering flames of burning torches set into the walls of the long corridor at regular intervals.

The figure suddenly stopped dead in its tracks.

Mike knew somehow that the weird swordsman had spotted him and his bowels turned to water. He was not only scared of the huge sword, but the weirdness of the whole impossible scene as well. There was quite plainly something supernatural going on here, and the occult was one of the few things that could really frighten Mike.

The hooded stranger shouted something that sounded like a

profanity, and then he charged down the corridor, swinging the sword above his head in a threatening gesture. Mike ran straight out of the room and burst into the bedroom, making Laura jump with fright. 'Stay there! It's someone with a sword!' he shouted, and he began to ramble and say incomprehensible things as he dragged a cabinet across the room to ram against the door.

'What's going on?' Laura shrieked, and Mike told her to call the police, but she couldn't find her mobile, not yet aware that she had left it in the spare room. Mike had left his phone in the kitchen after texting an apology to Pete Hammond earlier in the evening.

A gruff voice speaking in an unknown language said something immediately outside the bedroom door, and Laura screamed. Mike swore at the eerie intruder and claimed that he had just called the police. There was a pause of absolute silence for a few heartbeats, and then something struck the door with a terrific force which sent Laura into another fit of screams.

The tip of a blade – a sword's blade – shot through the door, just a few inches whilst the figure outside continued to batter the door for what seemed like an eternity. Mike ended up tipping over the wardrobe so that it crashed down on top of the cabinet already jammed against the door. In panic he looked desperately for his phone, and instead found an old Motorola mobile which flipped open, but of course, it hadn't been charged for years and Mike had no idea where the charger was. The doorknob rattled, and the stranger resumed his battering on the door for a further minute.

And then a tense silence descended upon the house.

Mike and Laura didn't dare move from that room until it was almost 7am, and when they did finally step out on to the landing, they expected to be confronted by the mad sword-wielding monk, but fortunately, he had gone. Having made it downstairs, Mike talked Laura out of calling the police and explained exactly where that psychopathic 'apparition' had come from – the mural. Laura wouldn't believe him until he insisted, 'Laura, I swear on my life! I swear on your life too, Laura, that thing came out of that corridor in the painting.'

Pete Hammond told the couple they could stay at his while he went to work that morning. Mike was in no mood to work, and nor was Laura. She sat there all day, saying hardly a word.

Pete Hammond bravely went over to Mike and Laura's house at 5.30pm and found it exactly as they had left it when they fled. But up in the spare room, he saw something very odd. The trompe-l'oeiul had now faded, and was barely visible, and someone had hacked up all the black bin liners full of scraped-off wallpaper. Pete examined their bedroom door and saw the blade marks where someone had struck out with a sharp weapon of some sort.

Somehow Pete managed to coax Mike and Laura back into their house. He also said he would personally paint over the strange painting in the spare room, and true to his word, he did. Even so, Laura began to have a series of nightmares in which she was dismembered in her bed by the weird swordsman, and in the end, the couple put the house up for sale.

As far as I know, the present occupants have not heard or seen anything strange at the Walton terraced house. I have researched the history of the house and found no evidence of any occultism relating to the premises. A wine merchant lived on there for 20 years in Victorian times, but he seems to have been a very upright and well-respected member of the community, although he was cousin to a herbalist named Henry Shuttleworth, who was known to be related to a family of alleged witches in the Liverpool of the 1850s.

We may find out more about the artist behind the chilling trompe l'oeiul one day.

THE PURPLE SHADES

I have a folder bulging with local unexplained mysteries in my study, and many of them have never been in print. Here's just one story from that folder, which came my way via an interview with the Allerton businessman (now retired) who is featured in this strange account.

One wintry Saturday afternoon in December 1974, successful Allerton businessman we shall call Richard Hamlyn, was browsing the television sets in the Radio Rentals shop on Garston's Speke Road. His wife had been constantly nagging him to replace their little black and white telly with a colour model, and now Richard had seen one with a 22-inch screen which would undoubtedly impress her. It would make an ideal Christmas gift for his wife. Richard realised he had insufficient funds in his wallet for the purchase, and so he nipped into the Garston Branch of the Liverpool Savings Bank, which was practically next door to the television shop.

After withdrawing enough money, he thought he would phone his Allerton home to see if his wife was still at work. He hoped she would be out so he could surprise her with the new telly. Richard entered one of the two red phone boxes outside the bank, dialled his home number, and a childish smirk broke out on his face when the phone just rang and rang. As he replaced the receiver, he noticed a curious pair of spectacles with amethyst-coloured lenses and solid silver frames and arms which someone had left on the telephone directory on the ledge of the callbox. He knew it was wrong, but he pocketed the specs and left the phone box to buy the television set. Within fifteen minutes, a taxi had taken him and the new television home. Muriel loved the set, and that Saturday evening watched *Tom and Jerry*, Bruce Forsyth in *The Generation Game, Doctor in Clover* – a comedy film starring Leslie Phillips, a Petula Clark Christmas Special, and a seasonal episode of *Kojak* – all in glorious vivid colour.

Richard, meanwhile, had made a chilling discovery when he looked through those pilfered purple-lensed spectacles. He was able to see ghosts through them! He doubted his sanity at first when he tried them on and looked out from his study window at the churchyard across the street and a 1950s-style teddy boy kept walking in and out of the cemetery through the solid railings. The apparition would also occasionally walk deliberately through passers-by, and some would actually react by halting for a moment or shuddering, and the ghost seemed to get a kick out of this effect he could induce in the living. Beads of sweat popped from Richard's brow when he discovered the ghost could only be seen through the purple shades. He didn't fancy telling Muriel about the unearthly glasses because she was terrified of anything of a supernatural nature.

Richard walked the dog that night, and when he came down Hillfoot Road, he decided to take the spectacles out of his inside jacket pocket and survey the nightscape all around. The place was teeming with a variety of figures who could only be ghosts, because they vanished when he peered over the rim of the violet-tinted lenses. He saw how some of the ghosts were dressed in sombre black Victorian and Edwardian clothes, while others were dressed in the fashions of his own time – so these were obviously the recently deceased. As he continued on his way, he realised that the phantoms were congregated around the nearby cemetery. He also noticed how Jake, his Welsh corgi, was reacting to their movements.

A girl of about 20 in a white tee shirt featuring a smiley face and a pair of green flared trousers, pranced past Richard, obviously assuming he could not see her as she skipped along, and Richard thought he could see a bloodstain on the back of her tee shirt. He stopped, rather spooked by the stain, and took off the glasses. All the way home, Jake kept turning round to look at something and sometimes he would growl at whatever it was. Richard prayed it was just a cat following him and his dog.

That night, Muriel went to bed square-eyed around 1am, and Richard sat up in the lounge, nursing a glass of brandy, pondering the effect of extraordinary spectacles. He rose from his chair and closed the curtains; there was the teddy boy across the road, standing outside the cemetery. Richard reached up to his eyes, thinking he had the glasses on for a moment, but soon realised they were on the table, and he went cold inside. He closed the curtains tight and then sat in his easy chair, trembling. A sudden thump to his right, and the door to the lounge creaked open by about 45 degrees. The thing perched on the top of that door almost triggered a cardiac arrest in the businessman. A wizened little woman with straggly, wet-looking hair, and a grotesque shrivelled face, looked down at him. She had on a dirty chestnut-brown garment of some sort, and her face was between her knees somehow. Her bony-fingered hands were clasped together. Her bare feet, with black pointed toenails, were gripping the top of the door's edge like long misshapen hands.

Richard was so afraid he could neither speak nor move. The ghoul pointed to him, then beckoned him with a curling forefinger as she cackled.

Richard threw the brandy glass at the entity and it bounced off her face and landed in shards upon the stereo record player.

'What was that? Richard?' came Muriel's voice from the bedroom.

Richard was so afraid, he found himself clambering out of the lounge window into the garden, where he ran off in a confused state, and by this time a hoar frost had formed on the pavement, so he slid about in his bewildered retreat, and almost fell over as he ran across the road – straight into the path of the teddy boy, who had an astonished look on his pallid face. 'Can you see me, Dad?' he asked a horrified Richard. 'Get away from me!' Richard screamed, and when he ran back across the road, he saw a highly-concerned Muriel in her nightdress, standing on their doorstep. He ran to her, and gave a garbled account of what was going on. Muriel smelt the brandy on his breath and advised him to come straight to bed.

For a few terrifying hours, Richard would occasionally glimpse the decrepit female ghoul and the teddy boy in the bedroom, barely visible by the lamp-post light shining weakly through the net curtains. Muriel embraced her trembling husband and prayed with him, even though she could not see or hear anything out the ordinary. She was seriously worried that he might be having a breakdown. At one point, the little ghoulish woman crawled on to the bed and Richard could feel her filthy damp dishevelled locks brushing against his forehead. Hair which reminded him of the disgusting heterogeneous mass of hairs that often collected in the bath plughole.

Somehow, Richard Hamlyn managed to fall asleep just after 4am, and he had a dream in which an unseen man with a very deep voice was urging him repeatedly to take the purple glasses back to that telephone call box on Speke Road. 'You're not supposed to see these things,' said the voice, adding, 'ignorance is bliss.'

Before breakfast that morning, Richard drove to the telephone box outside the Liverpool Savings Bank on Speke Road and left the accursed spectacles on the call-box shelf where he'd originally found them. He never saw the ghostly teddy boy after that, nor did he ever see that repulsive ghoul-like creature again either, and what's more, he never felt inclined to walk his dog again after dark.

So what were those purple spectacles which allowed Hamlyn to peer into the world of spirits that surround us? Well I believe the lenses were a vast improvement on the Kilner Screen, through which, people can purportedly see the human aura. The screen was invented by the British physician Walter J. Kilner (1847-1920), who practised at St Thomas's Hospital in London. Kilner believed the state of a patient's health corresponded with the changes in the colour and appearance of the (fabled) human aura – made visible through his light filter, which consisted of layers of glass between which he inserted a solution of dicyanin (a coal-tar derivative). Learned medical men of the day endorsed the Kilner Screen, and said it showed halos and auras around the human body, but someone in authority hampered its further development shortly after Kilner's death, and the screen vanished into obscurity.

The Soviet scientists Semyon Davidovich and his wife Valentina Khrisanova Kirlian later investigated the alleged human aura and managed to photograph it via a technique called electrophotography, although some scientists are yet to be convinced of the validity of Kirlian photography. Just who the absent-minded person was who left the purple-lensed glasses in that telephone call-box will probably never be known. I wonder who is in possession of the ghost glasses now ...

STRANGE ABDUCTIONS

From the following account and others of its inexplicable ilk, we may one day establish a scientific proposition, a lemma, which may form a stepping stone to some higher mathematical and dimensional truth currently unknown to us.

In 1986, the Conservatives decided that people who had been out of work for a specific period of time should be required to be interviewed as part of a return-to-employment scheme known as a Job Restart.

One blustery afternoon in March 1987, 21-year-old Garston woman, Jade, was called to such a Job Restart interview at Williamson Square Job Centre at 2.30pm. Jade got off the bus on Renshaw Street, and as she hurried along, she noticed an old woman trying to cross the busy road by Central Hall. The pensioner reminded Jade of her own late grandmother, so she pressed the button to the pelican crossing and then escorted the frail old lady to the other side. The old woman mumbled something which sounded like 'You'll do for me, love,' and then Jade looked at her watch and realised she had just ten minutes to get to her appointment.

Then Jade ran into something which she couldn't see, and at first it left her deaf. All the usual hubbub of Renshaw Street's traffic was no longer audible, and she found herself encased in something she subsequently described as 'a bubble'. She pressed her hands against the 'skin' of the invisible bubble. It felt like plastic, but it made her palms tingle. At first the bubble seemed to go down to the frightened girl's waist, so she could feel the wind on her bare legs, but then she felt the thing containing her move rapidly down her legs and slide under her heeled shoes. She cried out for help but the passers-by didn't seem to see or hear her. Then the mysterious bubble took on a slightly pinkish tint, and Jade began to feel dizzy and out of breath, and thought she was about to be suffocated. Her heart was thrumming and she began to hyperventilate. Her fists pounded on the unearthly membrane, and she frantically stamped her heels on the base of the thing, desperately hoping to puncture it. 'Oh God, please help me!' she screamed, and pushed with all her might against the walls of the rosy film.

Suddenly a hand grabbed her left forearm, and Jade turned to see the old woman she had helped across the road minutes before. She dragged Jade out of that bubble, and the girl felt her ears pop as the din of Renshaw Street returned. The pink bubble was now nowhere to be seen. Jade gulped the windy air and clung on to the old woman

– who was now studying her with an expression that Jade found very unsettling. She was grinning, and her eyes were of an unnatural indigo colour. Jade freed herself from her grasp and staggered off, sensing she was evil, and upon reaching Lewis's Corner, she looked back and saw the old woman had vanished.

To this day, Jade believes the old woman and that bubble were somehow connected. I have catalogued many of these 'bubble traps', as I call them, and have accounts of people stepping into them from eighteenth century Ireland to many local cases, of which Jade's is but one. Who sets the bubble traps and why? 'People-snatchers' from the future is my current theory, but that is all it is, pure conjecture with no hard evidence to back it up.

Going a little further back in time from what might have been some uncanny abduction attempt on Renshaw Street, we come to another incident which has eerie echoes of the 'bubble' incident. This particular episode took place one humid summer night in 1976, the year of a great drought in Britain. Mary, a mother in her thirties, was dozing next to her husband Bill at their three-bedroomed flat in St Oswald House, a tenement in Old Swan. The time was around half-past midnight and the couple were lying on top of the duvet with the windows wide open when they were suddenly startled by a scream from the bedroom of their only son, three-year-old Gareth. As they got up, ready to go his aid, Gareth burst into the bedroom and flung himself into his mother's arms. He was hysterical, but when his parents finally calmed him down, he said someone had pulled him out of his bed by his legs. The distressed lad's father, Bill, immediately went into Gareth's room and saw that his bedclothes had been scattered, but there was no sign of any intruder. Bill looked into every room in the house, before heading back to the bedroom where Mary and their little son were embracing on the bed.

Having found nothing to account for Gareth's fears, Bill decided he must have experienced a particularly vivid nightmare, and Mary suggested letting him sleep in their bed. 'No, once he starts that, he'll want to sleep in here every night,' Bill grumpily replied and he told Mary to go and lie with the boy in his room until he fell asleep. It took until around 2am for Gareth to fall asleep in his mother's arms in his own little bed.

He had been asleep for about five minutes when Mary decided to sneak away from the bed. As she tiptoed towards the door, she bumped into an invisible barrier. 'It was as if I had walked into a sheet of plate glass,' Mary told me. She reached out and her hands felt something cold and hard in front of her. Mary tried to walk away from the invisible obstruction, but the same thing happened again: an unseen barrier was blocking her way. As Mary's palms pushed against the infra-visible 'wall', which seemed to be curved, she suddenly noticed a fuzzy shadow appearing at the side of her son's bed. From this eerie shadow, two black silhouetted hands emerged and seized her sleeping son's ankles. The shadow entity then began to slowly pull Gareth into the amorphous black mass. Mary screamed and pounded her fists on the invisible partition, but her screams merely echoed back to her as if she was in a cave. The silhouetted hands continued to drag Gareth further into the undulating cloud of blackness until the child was engulfed in the ominous pall of darkness up to his chest.

Bill suddenly entered the bedroom and switched on the light, and immediately the black cloud evaporated, and Gareth fell from it and landed with a gentle thump at the side of his bed. Mary simultaneously discovered that the sinister invisible enclosure had vanished as mysteriously as it had first appeared, and she ran to Gareth's limp body lying on the floor. The boy was apparently unharmed, yawned grumpily as he was awakened by his frantic mother. Mary told her husband what had happened and for a while, Bill said nothing, but later that morning he admitted that he had seen the shadowy thing vanish in his son's room, a split second after he switched on the light. Mary was so afraid of the 'thing' returning, she moved Gareth's bed into the spare bedroom and would sit with him for over an hour each night after he had dozed off. But, fortunately, the family never experienced any further paranormal incidents in their flat.

When I was an 11-year-old altar boy, I overheard two priests chatting as I donned my black cassock and white cotta for the Mass.

The older priest was talking about a strange incident from his twenties, which would have been some time in the early 1950s. The priest told his younger colleague how he had been walking up Lime Street one evening during a torrential downpour, when he saw an old vagrant being ejected from the Crown Hotel by two men. The man was a known hellraiser who caused trouble wherever he went, and the priest had helped him on many occasions on condition that he would try and kick his drink habit.

On this rainy night, the priest had seen the vagrant stagger from the Crown, swearing loudly – then vanish into thin air. So abrupt was the vanishing act, the vagrant's speech was cut short mid-curse. Several passers-by also noticed the weird disappearance, and they slowed down and looked at the spot where the old vagabond had stood seconds before. The priest notified the police about the disappearing tramp but his report was not taken seriously, and the vagrant, apparently having no friends or family, was missed by nobody.

The old priest then told how, many years later, he was returning to Liverpool by train late one snowy evening. He had left Lime Street Station, and was hurrying to catch the last bus home, and on passing the Crown he and a passerby heard an elderly man's voice crying out for help. The priest instantly recognised the voice as that of the vagrant who had vanished on that part of Lime Street years before. He and the stranger tried to trace the source of the voice without success, and the priest, after many years of reflection, believed Satan had taken the drunk and imprisoned him in some sort of limbo.

The journalist and writer Ambrose Bierce, who vanished himself in mysterious circumstances, never to be seen or heard from again, in 1913, once wrote the following after reflecting on several cases of unexplained disappearances he had been researching:

Let us suppose that cavities exist in this otherwise universal medium, as caverns exist in the earth, or cells in Swiss cheese. In such a cavity there would be absolutely nothing. It would be such a vacuum as cannot be artificially produced; for if we pump the air from a receiver there remains the luminiferous ether. Through one of these cavities light could not pass, for there would be nothing to bear it. Sound could not come from it; nothing could be felt in it. It would not have a single one of the conditions necessary to the action of any of our senses. In such a void, in short, nothing whatever could occur. A man enclosed in such a closet could neither see nor be seen; neither hear nor be heard; neither feel nor be felt; neither live nor die, for both life and death are processes which can take place only where there is force, and in empty space no force could exist.

Around 1986, 41-year-old James left Rockfords pub (which is now Tso's Restaurant) on St John's Lane, in Liverpool city centre. James had only had a couple of pints and was not at all drunk. The time was 9.40pm and he was on his way to a chippy on Lime Street to get two mixed grills; one for him and one for his wife. Then he would go to the bus stop next to the Adelphi, on Brownlow Hill, to catch the 79 bus home to Netherley, where his pregnant wife Josie was waiting for him and, more importantly, her mixed grill.

As James was walking up St John's Lane, he thought he was going blind, because all of the street lights, traffic lights and vehicle headlamps began to fade, as if a thick fog was enveloping him. James unfurled a copy of the *Daily Mirror* he was holding and studied the headlines. They were clear enough, and with great relief James realised his eyes were fine but a dense fog was forming about him.

James then found himself in what he could only subsequently describe as a limbo of greyish green mist, through which a faint light was shining. All of the sounds of the city centre; the screech of bus brakes, the chatter and singing of revellers, and the constant faint bourdon note of incessant traffic in the distance, could no longer be heard. Instead, James could hear a very distant sound like a foghorn, which moaned through the mists as he walked around without any sense of direction. It was not long before he realised he was no longer in Liverpool, or at least the present-day Liverpool he knew. The ground was muddy and barely visible through the thick ground mist that swirled up to his waist.

James walked for miles and miles in search of a recognisable landmark, but found nothing: no roads, no pavements, just muddy ground and hills in a dirty green fog that would not thin. A length of time which James estimated to be an hour, at least, elapsed, and James began to cough as the cold mist aggravated his weak chest, and he began to feel worn out. As the mist thickened, the temperature dropped, and James delved into his jacket pocket, took out his lighter, and tightly screwed up his copy of the *Daily Mirror* into an ad hoc torch. He applied the blue and white flame of his Ronson lighter to the tip of the makeshift paper torch and carried on through the thick vapours holding the flaming torch before him.

And then he came upon vague shadows of people with their arms outstretched, accompanied by a multitude of groaning voices, but he could not make out a word of what was being said. James halted and saw dozens more shadows of these unknown people partially emerging from the fog, but their outlines looked almost fluidic, like watercolour renditions of the human form.

By now, James was convinced that someone had spiked his drink at Rockfords, because the whole experience seemed hallucinogenic, like some bad trip. He dropped the carbonised remains of his tabloid torch, panic setting in as the wailing sounds swelled the air behind him. At the bottom of some stone steps, James felt someone place what felt like a hand on his upper back, and in an instant all of the usual mundane lights and sounds of St John's Lane reappeared. He was in St John's Gardens. He was so afraid of venturing back into that terrifying limbo of weeping howling silhouettes, he walked the long way, around the back of St George's Hall, to get back to Lime Street, rather than take the more direct route to the chippy via St John's Lane. He told his wife about his bizarre excursion into some unknown fogbound place, and she could see that he was thoroughly upset. Then she also noticed mud stains on his shoes, socks and lower trousers, and most curious of all, a strange muddy handprint on the back of his jacket.

Had James somehow walked into a limbo of the lost? Thousands of people in Britain alone go missing every year, and whilst some of these people turn up again somewhere at some point, many are never seen again. I would not be surprised if a percentage of the missing are people who have literally vanished from our reality after walking into some other dimensional hell; some non-Euclidian no man's land between this world and God knows where.

Many years ago I interviewed a retired airline pilot who told me how, one afternoon in the 1990s, a jet – coming into Liverpool's airspace on a trajectory which would take it to the runways of Liverpool John Lennon Airport – suddenly vanished from the radar screens of air traffic control. It could not be seen visually and it was not present as a numbered target on the radar scopes. And then after about a minute, the plane reappeared on radar, and seconds later, it literally reappeared in the clear skies over southern Liverpool, and made a text-book landing. The pilot had not been aware of the break in communications between his plane and air traffic control, nor the mysterious radar and visual absence. But what if that plane full of passengers had vanished and not returned? Could it be that these disappearances, both temporary and permanent, are the work of some higher intelligence, or could it be down to some unfathomable force of nature? We may know more one day.

Some abductions, although not exactly paranormal, can be just as mysterious.

In the late 1970s in the Speke and Halewood areas of Liverpool, there were a number of attempted abductions of children and teenagers by a man dressed as a woman in outdated black attire which seemed to hark back to the 1940s and 1950s. This would-be abductor travelled about in a white sports car and spoke in a raspy voice as he pushed open the door of his car and pitched an invitation to his targeted victims. I remember an article about this strange miscreant in the *Liverpool Echo* and followed the case for a while, but the prospective abductor eventually disappeared into obscurity and fortunately was seen no more.

Going back further in time, to the 1920s, there was another menacing individual prowling the parks of Liverpool, attempting to snatch children in a very sinister way. I once received a handwritten letter from a delightful elderly woman named Peggy, who recalled how, around 1920, at the age of six, she had gone to Newsham Park to play with her best friend of the same age Mary Flannegan. At one point Mary went into the toilets, and about a minute afterwards, Peggy intended to follow her friend, but at the entrance to the toilets was a man dressed all in black. He wore a stylish bowler and sported a thick black walrus moustache and was carrying a sack over his shoulder. It was the type of sack Peggy had seen potatoes in at the grocers, and the man smiled down at Peggy as he adjusted the sack on his back.

Peggy noticed something was moving in the sack, and thought this was suspicious. The man hurried away and Peggy went into the toilets but Mary Flannegan was not inside. It then struck her what had happened – the man in the bowler had put Mary in the sack. She ran outside crying to passers-by, trying to tell them what had happened. Some of the people smiled and walked on, but one woman took Peggy's claims seriously and let her lead the way along a path until the little girl suddenly shrieked: 'There he is!' and she pointed to a man running near a bandstand, heading for a crowd of people. The woman gave chase and so did her younger male relative, causing the man to drop the sack and make a dash for it. The woman opened the sack and there was little Mary Flannegan, in a semi-conscious state. Her lips looked red, possibly burnt – which might have been caused by the administration of some sort of chloroform to render her unconscious. The abductor somehow managed to evade capture and the young man who had given chase later returned with his bowler hat. Mary Flannegan recalled nothing of her attempted abduction except a feeling of being suffocated (possibly caused by a chloroform-soaked handkerchief being pressed against her mouth).

Peggy recalled the abduction happening on the first of April, because some people were of the opinion that the whole incident had been some prank, but the police apparently took the case seriously and there were rumours that the child abductor had lived as a lodger at a house on Withers Street, within a stone's throw of the park. There were apparently other unsuccessful attempts to abduct children by the sack-man in both Wavertree Park and Sefton Park. Peggy recalled how the attempted Newsham Park abduction had prompted her mother to sing *The Ballad of Madge Kirby* as she was putting clothes through the mangle in the yard not long after the incident, and when Peggy asked who Madge was, her mother said: 'She was another little girl who was put in a sack, and she never saw her mother and father again.' Peggy's mother was, of course, referring to the mysterious murder of Madge Kirby, who was snatched from the streets of Kensington in January 1908. Her body was later found in a sack outside of a condemned house on Great Newton Street. The killer was never brought to justice, although I have presented a credible suspect in my book, *Murders Of Merseyside*.

CARNATES

One Saturday, in September 2012, I popped into the Midland pub on Ranelagh Street to research a haunting that was alleged to be taking place on the premises, and I spoke to several witnesses who saw a particular small round table tip itself over and throw several full glasses of lager over a customer. One witness was Ray, a fascinating debonair man in his seventies, who, with his lovely sister, nicknamed Toots told me some fabulous spooky tales of the pub that will no doubt find their way into print in my books one day. The table-tipper of the Midland is a discarnate ghost, it has no physical body, but some of the most frightening ghosts haunting this city are the carnates – ghosts that look as solid and real as you and I.

Now, some bizarre things have taken place in operating theatres. Years ago, in 1982, there was a case, thankfully not in Liverpool, where a patient woke up during an operation and, despite having a mask pumping anaesthetic over his mouth, began to sing the Eddy Grant hit, *I Don't Wanna Dance* at the top of his voice. Luckily the patient was given more gas and slipped back into unconsciousness. There was a report in the *Daily Mirror*, dated 17 January 1989, of an 82-year-old cancer sufferer exploding on an operating table. This took place as surgeon Jonathan Earnshaw was operating on the man at a Nottingham hospital. Electro-surgery was being used at the time and it is thought that an electrical spark might have caused gases containing methane in the pensioner's stomach to ignite and combust. The explosion was so loud, it was heard in the adjoining room of the theatre, but luckily the patient was not at all harmed, because, as Mr Earnshaw explained, 'the blast exploded outwards rather than inwards, otherwise the patient could have been killed.' The surgeon informed the *British Medical Journal* of the freak occurrence, which was the second recorded case of its kind. Mr Earnshaw had previously used the electrosurgery method 200 times without incident.

An even stranger incident occurred in a Liverpool operating theatre in the 1970s. The operation, to remove a length of bowel that was turning gangrenous, was literally touch and go, and at the most crucial stage, the surgeon noticed someone looking over his right shoulder, though the nurses saw nothing. The surgeon turned to find a naked man, and a very familiar one at that; it was the very patient on the operating table – his exact double.

'Please don't let me die,' he muttered, and seemed horrified as he looked down at his flesh-and-blood body which had been opened to show the internal organs. Surgeons are renowned for nerves of steel and remaining cool under the most trying circumstances, and this surgeon knew he was seeing what his colleagues had reported from time to time – some sort of projected doppelganger of the person being operated on.

'It isn't nice being dead,' said the apparently solid-looking carnate apparition, and he began to tremble. The surgeon did his best to ignore the eerie figure and continued the operation, but some of the theatre staff noticed that he had been distracted by something. A few minutes later, the carnate 'ghost' cried out and vanished, and the lights flickered in the operating theatre. The man on the operating table died – but was successfully resuscitated – and after he had made a full recovery, he told the surgeon how he had 'fallen' out of his body and gone into the depths of Hell for a while, where he saw all kinds of terrifying demons and 'bad-looking people' screaming, and then he had somehow floated back up into this world, where he realised he was merely a ghost who could only observe. The surgeon was fascinated, especially when the patient suddenly said: 'I stood next to you and watched you operate on my guts. You saw me, didn't you? It was too real to be a dream.'

The surgeon – a man of science and logic who believed death meant total annihilation of consciousness and the self – wanted to admit that he had seen his patient's 'wraith' or doppelganger as the Occultists of old called such projections of the etheric body, but instead, perhaps fearing he would lose his job, and that colleagues would question his sanity, he told the patient that the anaesthetic had probably caused him to have a very lucid dream. Secretly though, the incident made him question all he had previously believed about a life in the hereafter.

Incidentally, many hospitals have now put labels with codes and symbols which are stuck on top of lockers and other out-of-sight places in wards, and patients who have reported out-of-body experiences have reportedly seen these hidden labels. A hospital in Southampton was one of the first to experiment with the labels because of the sheer number of near-death-experiences reported by patients who had 'died' during operations and then been resuscitated.

In the mid-1990s, two students in their early twenties, Rhiannon and Katy, who were both from the Netherton area, decided to share a tiny first floor flat at a rather secluded location in Liverpool city centre. The flat was on Hockenhall Alley, a shadowy passageway off Dale Street which time has forgotten. The grim-looking alley runs between Vernon Street and Cheapside like some anachronistic Dickensian lane from the old East End of London.

The students had only been at the Hockenhall Alley flat for just over a week when something quite eerie took place. It was a hot summer evening, and Katy and Rhiannon were having difficulty sleeping. The girls lay on their beds in their underwear reading magazines with the radio on low. Katy thought she saw something move out of the corner of her right eye, and turned towards the open window. She could have sworn she had seen a man's head with white hair duck down, but thought this was unlikely – unless he was a

Peeping Tom on a ladder, as the window was 18 feet above the pavement. And so Katy returned to her magazine, and Rhiannon was saying she wasn't sure which pop-singer she liked more; Liam Gallagher of Oasis or Damon Albarn of Blur when she suddenly let out a yelp.

Rhiannon dropped her magazine and found Katy sitting up, transfixed as she gazed in horror at the window.

'What?' was all Rhiannon could manage, and she followed Katy's line of sight, but could see nothing at the window.

'There was an old man looking in at me!' Katy said, putting on a baggy white tee shirt as she got up.

Rhiannon smiled uneasily and went to the window.

'Don't, Rhi!' Katy shrieked, but her friend was already at the window, and without looking out to see if there was anybody down on the pavement, she closed it and fastened it securely, even though the room was stiflingly hot.

Katy insisted she had seen a man's weathered, well-tanned face with contrasting white hair and ice-blue eyes at the open window. He had been ogling her. 'You sure you didn't doze off and dream him ...' said Rhiannon, 'just for a few seconds? I've done that many a time.'

'I didn't dream him. It was a dirty old man.'

'He must have long legs to be able to look into our flat!'

Rhiannon gave a false smirk, because she was trying to convince herself that the voyeur was all in her friend's mind. The idea gave her the creeps, but she wouldn't admit this to Katy.

That weekend the girls went out to a club called The State, which was just around the corner on Dale Street, and they got back home around 2.15am after getting kebabs. The alcohol and the sizzling temperatures led Rhiannon to throw open the bedroom window and then strip before lying down on the bed. Katy slept on top of her own bed in her underwear, singing herself to sleep.

At around 3.15am, Rhiannon woke. Someone was kissing her toes. She looked over to Katy's, and by the faint red indicator light of a muted radio, she could see her friend was sleeping face down. Rhiannon then looked down towards the bottom of her bed, where a stranger with shoulder-length white hair, knelt kissing her feet. She let out a scream, startling him, and then with amazing agility spurred by the sudden adrenalin rush, she flew across the room and slapped on the light-switch. For a second after the light came on, Rhiannon saw the figure of a shortish man running towards the window and then vanishing into thin air. She heard his footfalls, as did Katy, and then nothing.

It was obvious he was the same person Katy had seen peering in through the window a few days back. Katy closed the window, but the girls were so afraid of another encounter with the white-haired ghost, they spent the night in the living room. For just over a week, nothing unusual happened, but on the following Monday, while Rhiannon was showering one evening at around 11pm, the door to the bathroom slowly began to open and close. Through the misted panes of the shower cubicle Rhiannon watched, breathless, as the ghost entered the bathroom, this time wearing a peculiar black hat with a brim which curled up on either side. The hat together with the long white hair reminded Rhiannon of the man on the box of Quaker Oats porridge. The ghost came up close to the shower cubicle and pressed a hand on the pane as Rhiannon screamed and wet herself with fright. Her cries brought Katy running to the bathroom, but she saw no one. However, both girls did see the strange pale handprint of the 'Quaker' on one of the panes of the shower cubicle. It was powdery as if someone had coated their hand in talcum powder before leaving the impression. As the girls looked on in disbelief, the impression slowly faded away.

Understandably, Rhiannon and Katy abandoned the flat, which had been leased to them by an agency near Church Street, and they went back to the agency and demanded another flat and were given one in Old Swan.

I mentioned this case on a radio programme and received many calls, letters and emails about the ghost in question. Many of the listeners were sure that it was the ghost of an old puritan, Edward Moore, who was a Bible-basher by day and a Peeping Tom by night, infamous for prowling about and peeping through windows at the town's attractive womenfolk. He was also an infamous eavesdropper who knew everyone's business. When he died, people were glad to see the back of the self-righteous voyeur, but Moore's ghost was seen a few days after his burial, and even in death, he got up to his old tricks, listening at keyholes, peeping through windows at women as they took their fireside baths, and floating up to windows to spy on couples' love-making. What made this ghost seem even creepier was the way Moore seemed to be solid. He was supposedly chased down Hockenhall Alley one Christmas Eve in the 1950s and left shoe-prints in the snow, and when he vanished into a brick wall, his trail of sole-prints led straight into that wall.

One woman who got in touch with me told how, one morning at around 1.50am, in 2002, she desperately needed the toilet, and had to go far down Hockenhall Alley to urinate, in the middle of which she heard heavy breathing close by. Caught in such a compromising position, she felt more embarrassed at the thought of someone standing nearby than worried as to who that person might be. And then she saw a man in a long black coat stepping out of a doorway. He also wore white tight-fitting stockings and square-toed buckled shoes. The woman couldn't see the stranger's face, but she couldn't miss his long white straggly hair. He bent over her, and sensing he was not a modern person but a ghost, she pulled up her knickers and ran off screaming down the street.

Another realistic-looking carnate apparition haunted the Merseyside Ambulance Training School in Woolton's Quarry Street for many years, and some tell me that it is still at large. I am referring to the manifestations of a policeman in an old-fashioned uniform who has been seen in the Ambulance Training School and in the surrounding district, mostly during the hours of twilight. Jim, who was employed at the training school, told me how one evening when he was working late he heard heavy footsteps in the corridor outside one of the lecture rooms. He was surprised because he assumed he was alone in the school, and so he gingerly opened the door a few inches and peeped out to find a tall broad-shouldered policeman marching along the well-lit corridor. Jim followed him, but then the figure vanished, along with the heavy footfalls, leaving an eerie silence to fall on the premises. Jim soon abandoned his work, locked the place up and left.

Jim told a colleague about the ghostly policeman and his friend said he had seen him twice himself, and on the second occasion he had actually bumped into the copper as he turned a corner into a corridor at the school. Many of the locals in the area have also seen the stocky policeman walking about, including an elderly woman who asked the policeman if he had the right time. He walked on along Linkstor Road, and then vanished into thin air.

Perhaps we should not be too surprised at the constable from beyond, because the Merseyside Ambulance Training School was once a police station. As recently as August 2011, I had a report from a taxi driver who told me how he had almost run down the spectral policeman on Woolton's Church Road. He only realised the policeman was a ghost when he saw him fade away as he walked towards the roundabout on Beaconsfield Road.

I personally recall an incident which fits in well in this chapter. One blustery March night in 2002 my friend Liam bumped into his old mate Carl, who he had not seen for seven years. The chance encounter took place on Lawrence Road in Wavertree, and the two men shook hands and chatted. Carl asked Liam if he had 40pence to make a phonecall. Liam offered Carl his mobile but Carl said he didn't want the people he was calling to have his number and insisted on making the call from a callbox. Liam gave him a pound, as he had no small change. He then told Carl he would be in the nearby pub – the Salisbury. After about half an hour, closing time was looming and Liam wondered where Carl had got to and so he left the Salisbury and went to the telephone callbox, which was only about 30 yards away, and found a single pound coin on the ledge inside the box.

Liam later discovered that Carl had died on that very date in March from a heart attack – three years before! He told a member of Carl's family and straight away, this person asked Liam: 'Did he ask you for money to make a call?' Liam nodded, and was told that on the day he became seriously ill, Carl tried to phone his mother rather than dial 999 for an ambulance. His body was later found in a certain telephone call box in Wavertree. Carl's ghost had asked many other people if he could borrow money for a call – a call he never makes.

Why these carnate ghosts do this is a mystery. Is it a type of psychosis? Are the dead attempting to come to terms with a sudden death? Or is it a form of attention seeking to make the living acknowledge a lonely soul trapped between worlds? It is chilling to think that we may know from first-hand experience one day.

BEYOND THESE PRISON WALLS

In the early 1960s, 22-year-old Graham from Wavertree was sentenced to three years in Walton Prison for aggravated burglary, and he found himself sharing a cell with a man in his early sixties named Arthur. Arthur was a very quiet, serious individual who didn't take to well to his new cellmate at first, as Graham was very talkative and quick to anger, and forever complaining about his situation and how the warders treated him. Arthur advised Graham to take up meditation, and in the early 1960s, the concept of meditation was not as widely known as it is today. Initially, Graham scoffed at the idea of 'sitting cross-legged to have a light nap' – which is how he described the practice, but eventually, Arthur taught the young man that his worst enemy was his negative outlook and restless mind. Arthur hinted that he had learned some mysterious esoteric secrets, and would often spend a lot of time laying out Tarot cards on his bed which he would then muse upon for hours. He also practised what seems to have been an advanced form of yoga, and for a man in his sixties he was able to flex his limbs into positions which Graham found impossible to imitate. He taught Graham how to increase the range of his hearing, so the young inmate could listen in on conversations taking place quite a distance away in another part of the prison.

But Arthur's greatest talent came to light one day when Graham became bored reading a book. He jumped off his bunk and was about to tap Arthur on his arm, when he noticed that his cellmate looked very pale. Graham listened carefully and was sure Arthur was not breathing. He placed his hand on his chest – no heartbeat. He felt for a carotid pulse – there wasn't one.

At this point one of the warders was passing the cell, so Graham banged on the cell door.

'What's up?' said the warder.

'I think me mate's snuffed it!' Graham shouted, and then came a rattle of keys in the lock. The warder came in, and seeing Arthur looking pale and lifeless, smiled, then turned to Graham and said, 'Nah, he's not dead, laddie, he's gone off on one. He's always doing this. He'll be back soon. Don't wake him... he says its dangerous to wake him when he's like this.'

Graham returned a perplexed look as the warder left the cell and locked up.

About 15 minutes elapsed, and then Arthur opened his eyes and suddenly took a sharp intake of breath.

'I thought you were dead, you old duffer!' Graham told the old lag, and a faint smile broke out on Arthur's face, 'I was.'

'What?'

'I had a holiday from my self, and then I went roaming about,' Arthur claimed. And then in some detail he explained how he had projected his 'Astral Body' out of his normal flesh and blood body to leave the prison. He had floated across Walton and drifted high over the River Mersey to visit the house of a cousin in North Wales. He had floated about in the garden and appreciated the spectrum of coloured flowers in the sunlight. It had been an exhilarating feeling of pure freedom which contrasted so strongly against confinement in a grey prison cell with niggling arthritis.

'Please teach me how to do what you did,' Graham begged, but Arthur said Astral Travelling was a dangerous practice, because sometimes a person could become stuck and find themselves unable to get back into their corporeal body, and on some rare occasions, demonic entities could get into the vacant earthly body and squat in it, causing a type of possession. Graham said the risks were worth taking for the ability to travel out of the prison and enjoy the ultimate freedom of travelling wherever one wanted to go in the world.

For nigh on a fortnight Graham badgered Arthur to teach him the art of Astral Projection, until at last, the elder relented and said he would teach him the rudimentary techniques to get him started. These lessons would have to be taught after 'lights out' when the cells were plunged into darkness each night, otherwise the warders would interrupt the deep meditative state needed for the projection of the Astral body.

One warm August night at around 11.45pm, with his eyes gently closed, Graham willed his mind's eye out of his ultra-relaxed body, and saw the high barred window of the cell in front of him, just as if he was looking at it with his eyes wide open. He drifted through the window and hovered over the sheer drop into the yard below. He saw the walls of the prison clearly and the twinkling lights of the street lamps and the myriad coloured squares of people's curtained windows all about. He drifted like a soap bubble across Hornby Road but soon lost his bearings, as he was not only unaccustomed to seeing the streets of Liverpool from such a height, it was also night-time, and so it was hard to pick out any landmarks to navigate by. He drifted higher and higher, and gradually found himself travelling eastwards over Fazakerley, and then the world below was nothing more than a constellation of lights. Some were moving as pinpoints of light – the headlamps of vehicles travelling along the East Lancs.

And then, as Graham estimated he was somewhere over Prescot, a terrifying roar filled his ears, and he turned to see a monster flying towards him. It was an airliner hurtling towards him, and it was so close, he could see the pilot and air-crew in the dimly-lit cockpit. The tip of the plane's wing sliced through Graham where his somatic torso would have been, but he felt nothing – no pain at all, just pure fear. The airliner continued on its journey through the night, possibly from Manchester to Ireland. The 'mid-air collision' scared Graham so much, he willed himself back to Walton Prison, and immediately he felt himself being tugged towards the west. He slanted down through the night air until he began to recognise some landmarks: Aintree Racecourse to his right and to the south west was Walton Hall Park.

He wished himself at a lower altitude and found that action followed thought almost immediately. All the time Graham wondered if this was all some dream, and this was at the back of his mind until he suddenly woke up on his bunk with Arthur kneeling beside him looking concerned.

'You did it then?' he asked, then smiled.

Graham swore, and then said: 'It was great! I want to do it again!'

But Arthur advised against another trip so soon after the last one. 'You're still a novice, Graham. What we'll do tomorrow night is go out together.'

'What?' Graham asked, unsure of how his friend's suggestion might work.

'We'll both project and you'll feel more confident with another person around,' Arthur explained.

Graham shook his hand and then within 15 minutes, was fast asleep, drained by his Astral maiden voyage.

At around 11pm on the following evening, Arthur lay, as usual, on the top bunk and Graham lay stretched out on the bottom one. Both men had gone through the same deep relaxation technique which had also slowed down their heart rate to well below normal. The resting heart rate of the average person can be 100 to 60 beats per minute, but through Arthur's breathing and visualisation technique, he had brought his heart rate below 28 beats per minute. Such slowness of the heart is known as Bradycardia, a condition that can lead to death in some people. Graham found himself soaring high above the grim confines of the prison, and on this occasion he could see the misty form of Arthur's Astral body beside him. Arthur's etheric form looked just like a naked human body, only it was partially transparent and had a blue phosphorescent glow to it. When Graham heard Arthur's voice, he heard it in his mind, as if by telepathic communication.

The two temporarily-free prisoners drifted south towards Anfield and Arthur led Graham down to rooftop level, where an attic window was lit up. A young woman was sitting up in the attic bedroom, reading a magazine as she listened to the transistor radio.

Arthur went through the attic window as if it were as solid as a ray of light, and Graham followed. Graham wondered why his guru had brought him into this place. He found the woman extremely attractive, even though she was wearing men's pyjamas.

'Watch this,' Arthur's voice sounded in Graham's mind. Arthur inhaled and then began to blow his breath on to the girl's face. She was, of course, unaware of her two invisible observers. Her fringe moved with his exhaled breath, and she shuddered slightly as she experienced the draught across her face. Arthur then passed his hands back and forth over the transistor radio several times, creating spooky-sounding howls of interference to exude from the radio's loudspeaker. The woman looked quizzically at the radio and then Arthur said, 'Right, young Graham, let's be on our way,' and readied himself to leave the cramped attic lodgings belonging to a woman he had seen many times on his travels out of his body.

It had been a while since Graham had been in the company of women since he'd been sentenced, and he could not resist kissing her on the cheek.

As she felt the kiss the woman screamed, which startled Graham, but Arthur was intrigued, for she had actually felt the kiss. Graham obviously had a talent that was very rare – he was able to influence physical objects when he was in the Astral state. Arthur worried that someone as undisciplined as Graham might misuse his talent and possibly assault any woman that took his fancy during his travels from now on.

The woman fled the room, probably thinking a ghost had caressed her face, and Arthur urged Graham to leave the attic immediately. Graham did this and he and his cellmate were soon gliding again across the rooftops of moonlit Liverpool. Graham said it was such a lovely feeling to kiss a woman after being cooped up in a cell for so long, but Arthur strongly advised him not to take advantage of his unusual ability again, for he would succumb to the dark, lustful side of his mind, and could end up becoming some sort of perverted predator. Graham said nothing in reply. The astral excursion soon ended, and the two men returned to their respective bodies in the prison cell, exhausted by the trip, and both slept soundly that night.

On the following day around noon, Graham was having dinner with the other prisoners, when he suddenly felt a sharp stabbing pain in his lower abdomen. It became so intense he almost threw up and collapsed. Appendicitis was naturally suspected and Graham was taken to Walton Hospital. It was indeed appendicitis, and after the operation, Graham woke up in bed, feeling terribly groggy as the effects of the anaesthetic began to wear off. As he lay there with nothing to do, he decided he would astrally project himself, and this time he managed to come out of his body during the hours of daylight. He flew up from the hospital and travelled miles until he came to a school playground. Watching the children at play was a blonde female teacher with a very shapely figure, and Graham, full of desire, floated down out of the sky, and circled her. He moved in and gave the woman a full kiss and ran his hands all over her. The woman recoiled in horror at the invisible assailant and hurried into the building – and Graham followed her.

A red-headed woman of a similar age – the school secretary, came out of her office and the young teacher told her what had just happened. As the secretary shot a faintly bemused look at the teacher, Graham decided to kiss the redhead's neck, and she emitted a squeal of surprise, which made the teacher jump as well. Graham wanted to throw his arms around the necks of the teacher and the secretary and kiss them both again, but a priest suddenly came down the corridor, and Graham felt guilty at the sight of the man of the cloth, so he flew along the corridor and out of the hallway until he was floating just above the playground again. He then rose to rooftop level and everything went out of focus. He was back in the hospital bed. A nurse had woken Graham to give him some painkillers.

Graham then fell asleep, but when he awoke it was getting dark, and the ward was silent except for the padding to and fro of a night nurse doing her rounds. It must have been around 10.30pm when Graham travelled out of his body again, and this time he wandered across the skies of the city and found himself drawn to the Wavertree area, and a stretch of Smithdown Road in particular which was swarming with young attractive women. Graham floated down to a popular music venue of the time called Holyoake Hall, off Smithdown Road and Blenheim Road.

A beautiful red-head was standing outside the Holyoake, apparently being pestered by two men in black leather jackets and jeans who looked as if they were trying to chat her up. The girl tried to move away from them but one of the pests blocked her way and leaned against the wall, barring her way with his arm. At this point, Graham wanted to strike out with his fist at the yob but decided to try an experiment. With every ounce of his willpower, he focused on the head of the youth pestering the girl and with laser concentration, urged him to walk away – and to Graham's utter surprise, the young man suddenly turned around and walked away without a word, much to the bafflement of his friend and the red-headed girl.

This would prove to be a turning point in Graham's sinister career, for now he realised he could actually influence people's behaviour through his extraordinary gift.

There was a loud beep, a screech of tyres, a scream from the red-head and a loud thud.

The youth in the leather jacket who had been telepathically instructed to walk away had walked blindly into the path of a Hackney cab. His body was thrown about 20 feet into the air and landed with a sickening smack on the cold tarmac. A crowd appeared out of nowhere and gathered around the lifeless body which had rolled into the gutter. Graham floated over the heads of the morbid spectators and noticed blood streaming down a grid, and then came a voice from someone within the crowd: 'God, you can see his brains. He's a goner.'

'His leg's shaking look,' said a female voice.

'That's just nerves … he's dead,' said a mature male voice.

'He just walked out in front of me as if he was in a trance!' the taxi driver cried.

Graham flew skywards and returned to his body which was lying in the darkened ward in Walton Hospital. He woke up in tears. He felt as if he had just murdered an innocent young man. He felt so nauseous and racked with guilt. He wanted to talk to Arthur so badly for advice, and considered projecting himself to the prison to contact his mentor but found himself too weak to do so and eventually he fell into a fitful sleep.

Several days later, just before Graham was transferred back to his prison cell, he read in a copy of the *Liverpool Echo* how a youth had been left with serious head injuries after being knocked down by a taxi on Smithdown Road outside the music and dance venue Holyoake Hall. Graham's heart skipped a beat as he read how the youth had been hit after leaving his older sister and brother at the dance hall. So had the red-head been the accident victim's older sister? Had he got it all wrong?

Despite his shame and guilt, a tempting possibility came into Graham's mind: could he control a person – just as he had caused that youth to walk into the road – to such an extent, that the person could steal for him? He knew it was a despicable thought, but he nevertheless visualised some innocent person robbing a bank for him, and stashing the loot away for him for when he came out. Before long he had begun to scheme about all the criminal possibilities of being able to astral project, say into banks to observe the combinations of safes.

An icy cold chill coursed down Graham's spine. He felt like superman with this new power, and then another sickening thought entered his mind; could he somehow get sexual gratification from a woman – any woman – he chose to target whilst in his astral form? Knowing very well that this amounted to a form of rape, he couldn't banish the thoughts from his mind.

When he finally arrived back in his cell, he confessed these appalling thoughts to Arthur, and even admitted that, although he was ashamed of them, he was worried he'd carry them out, because it was just such a lack of self-control in the past that had resulted in him being put behind bars. Whilst Arthur admired his honesty, and was glad he had come clean about his shockingly shameful thoughts, he also said something which really frightened Graham: 'I can see something else in there as I look into your eyes.' Then Arthur scrutinised his inmate's face in such an intense way it made his blood run cold.

'What do you mean "something else"?'

'While you've been projecting, something out of this place has slipped in there, and it's trying to turn you.'

'You mean possession?' Graham asked, his mouth dry.

'Yes, I'm afraid so,' said Arthur. 'And it now knows that we know about it. Do you feel alright?'

'Yes, I feel alri...' Suddenly Graham collapsed on to his bunk, cracking the top of his head on the framework. He landed heavily, and began to shake.

Arthur bent over him and made the sign of the cross, touching Graham's forehead, the centre of his chest, and then his left and right shoulders with his index finger. 'Unclean spirit, I abjure thee and summon thee forth to leave this body in the name of Jesus Christ!'

Graham smiled, but Arthur knew that the smile was not the work of his cellmate, but of something evil which had infiltrated his mind.

'Jesus is Lord!' Arthur shouted at the inane grinning face.

Graham swore and described in stomach-churning detail the things he'd like to do to women.

'Jesus is Lord, and the Lord commands you to leave this work of his! This soul belongs to Jesus!' Arthur told the evil presence lurking in Graham.

'I am Astaroth! How can you make me leave?' Graham said in a low gruff voice quite unlike his own.

'You are not Astaroth or any other demon,' Arthur mocked. 'You're the pathetic dirty little spirit of someone who was hanged in here a long time ago!'

Then Graham's eyes flew open but those burning golden eyes were not his, but those of something truly repellant, full of unbridled hatred.

'In the name of the Archangel Michael, leave this man!' Arthur commanded, upon which Graham spat at him.

'Baalberith protects me! You'll die now! Die!' said the unearthly mocking voice.

'I command thee unclean spirit, in the name of the Father, of the Son, and of the Holy Ghost, to depart from this man whom Our Lord Jesus Christ has vouchsafed ...' Arthur was reciting, when Graham's eyes suddenly closed, and a black inky liquid dribbled out of his nostrils and pooled on the bedclothes. This pool of blackness then slithered quickly across the bed, dripped on to the cell floor, and vanished between the cracks in the tiles.

Graham woke a few minutes later with a severe headache, but at the same time feeling as if some great weight had been lifted from his shoulders. It was hard to define, but he felt physically and mentally lighter somehow. Arthur strongly advised his friend to refrain from astral travelling for a while, in case the prison spirit came back. But Graham had had enough of projecting himself out of his body, and instead, he took to reading the Bible every day. He volunteered for a job in the prison library and asked Arthur not to mention anything to do with the Occult again, and the old man complied with Graham's wishes.

Graham eventually left the prison and devoted a lot of his time to charity work. He said his personal 'road to Damascus' turning point came when he was possessed and shared the dark and desperate thoughts of a damned soul that wanted to do unspeakable evil to people – mostly women. He described how his soul had been in a type of hellish isolation, cut off from God, and he certainly didn't want to end up like that after death.

Astral travel is referred to in every culture on earth, and for those of you who would like to attempt it, the bookshops and the internet are laden with information on how to project the consciousness. I would particularly recommend the following two books for the would-be astral traveller: *The Projection of the Astral Body* by Sylvan Muldoon and Hereward Carrington, and *The Study and Practice of Astral Projection* by Robert Crookall. A word of warning though before you attempt this esoteric discipline. Catalepsy – the inability to move a single muscle – is sometimes experienced by the novice when he or she first attempts exercises freeing the astral body from the flesh and blood one, although this condition is usually just temporary and soon passes as the apprentice progresses. Good luck.

One more thing; in the 1980s there was a well-documented case of what seems to have been some form of astral projection which took place at Walton Gaol. A certain violent prisoner asked the prison authorities if he could attend his mother's funeral, but his request was allegedly rejected because in the past he had attempted to escape when he was given leave to visit his mother in hospital. The funeral went ahead and during the requiem service at a certain church in north Liverpool, the prisoner was seen by many kneeling alongside the mourners. This was not a case of mistaken identity, because the priest, who knew the prisoner well, even came down from his pulpit to get a better look at him. Some present thought the prisoner had escaped to attend the service for his mother, but when the priest approached him, he vanished in an instant, and this vanishing act disrupted the requiem mass for a while. The priest made enquiries and discovered that the prisoner had unquestionably been in his cell at the time of the service, kneeling at his bunk as he said a series of prayers for his mother. It was thought that the prisoner had had such a longing to attend his mother's funeral, he had somehow projected his astral form to the church, perhaps unknowingly.

THE FACE

In 1997, the Grand National was postponed when police acted on a coded bomb threat from representatives of the Provisional IRA. Believing bombs had been planted at the world-famous racecourse, the police and authorities evacuated some 60,000 spectators from the Aintree venue, as well as the jockeys, horses, trainers and other race personnel. People who had come to the Aintree racecourse in cars and coaches were forced to leave them in the rush, and the police then secured the course. With limited hotel accommodation in the city because of record visitors for the Grand National, the displaced racegoers from outside Liverpool naturally worried where they'd stay. Liverpool hospitality soon reared its head, and thousands of local residents in Aintree, and beyond, opened their doors and took in the stranded would-be race-goers. No bombs were found at the racecourse, and two days later, the National was run on a Monday, and the tabloids, for once, portrayed the kindness of Liverpool people in a positive manner in their features about the mass act of hospitality towards the tourists who would have otherwise been left high and dry by the effects of the bomb scare.

In 2005, charles, a Birmingham vicar, wrote to me to tell me of a very strange incident that occurred in Aintree during that weekend when the National was postponed. He and his wife Jane had arrived at Aintree in a coach – one of the vehicles that were secured by the police after the bomb alert. So he and his wife were not allowed back on to this coach, and soon found themselves looking for accommodation in the exodus from the racecourse. The couple were approached by an elderly kind-faced woman, probably in her mid to late seventies. Her name turned out to be Jean, and she told Charles and Jane that they would be more than welcome to stay with her until they could find accommodation or return home. The vicar offered to pay Jean for the inconvenience of having two strangers under her roof for a few days, but she wouldn't hear of it. She told them her home was no mansion, but a mere humble semi-detached house on Longmoor Lane (in nearby Fazakerley).

Charles and Jane were waited on by Jean, who cooked them a roast that eventful Saturday, and at around 8.30pm, Charles insisted on taking Jean and his wife to the nearest pub, and the trio enjoyed good conversation in the comfy parlour in front of an open fire.

At around 10.20pm, Charles, Jane and Jean returned to the house on Longmoor Lane, where they watched a little television and enjoyed a light supper put on by the unstinting Jean. By 11.35pm, Charles and his wife were about to go to bed, when they thought they heard footsteps going up the stairs and walking along the landing above. Jean seemed a bit jumpy and said that the sounds were from next door. 'These walls are paper thin,' Jean she said, and the couple thanked their host, and went up to the guest bedroom.

On reaching the landing, they saw the shadowy figure of a tall woman in very dark clothes flit past – and she seemed to pass through the guest bedroom door. Charles was standing behind his wife when the extraordinary sighting took place, and Jane had a better view of the apparent ghost than her husband, and she was sure that the figure had been wearing a bonnet or hat of some sort. The vicar was reluctant to enter the room, but he pushed the door open and turned on the light as quickly as possible – and found it empty.

The couple were soon in bed, and as there wasn't a bedside lamp in the room, the reverend opened the curtains wide and let the faint amber light of a street lamp post shine into the room. He lay in bed, and Jane mentioned the shadowy spectre she and Charles had seen minutes before, and whether it could have been nothing more than a reflection or a product of their overtired minds. Charles said nothing in reply. The couple embraced, and at around 1am they had fallen fast asleep.

At 3am exactly, Jane woke, and squinted, fuzzy-eyed at her wristwatch on the bedside cabinet to note the time. She heard a noise in the bedroom, a rustle of fabric, and then silence again. This happened three times. Then she heard breathing close by. It was not her husband, as he was lying face down in the pillow with the blankets almost covering his head. Where then, was this rhythmic breathing noise coming from? Jane thought she felt breath on her right ear, as if someone was behind her. She slowly lifted herself up from the pillow and turned to look at the headboard – and there, protruding from the wall, was the pallid face of a woman with huge black staring eyes.

Jane almost threw herself out of bed, and she staggered towards the light switch. A dismal low-wattage bulb burned in a light shade dangling from the low ceiling – and now there was no sign of that ghastly-looking female face.

Jane woke her husband and told him what she had seen and was so afraid she swapped places with him so that he now slept on the side of the bed where the eerie face had materialised.

The couple slept soundly, and there were no more paranormal incidents that night. However, on the following night, again as the couple were retiring to their room, they both saw the same ghostly dark figure of a tall woman who fled as they reached the top of the stairs, and this time she lingered a second or so longer before flitting through the solid door to the guest bedroom. Charles thought the apparition was Edwardian with its hat and ankle length dress, but Jane thought it could have equally been Victorian in origin. The vicar and his wife slept with the light on that night, and at around four in the morning, Jane opened her eyes to see the ghostly woman's face frowning at her close up, the chalk-white deathly pallor of the face contrasted against the ghost's huge jet black eyes. Jane slowly reached towards her husband under the covers but his hand clutched hers – for he was already awake, and he whispered, 'Don't be afraid, Jane.'

He too had seen the ghost. He had been awakened earlier when he felt the mattress sink down as the woman in black sat close to his feet watching them.

Jane screwed up her eyes and screamed: 'Go away!'

And then she felt a cold breeze against her face. When she opened her eyes, the ghost had gone.

Enough was enough. The couple got dressed, sneaked downstairs and stayed in the kitchen until Jean rose and joined them at around 7.30am. Charles and Jane didn't like to mention the ghost in case it worried their host, and yet they suspected that Jean probably knew of the apparition's existence.

I tried to research this case, but unfortunately, when I visited the house in Fazakerley, I learned that Jean had long passed away and the house was in the process of being sold. The ghostly woman in black will probably continue to haunt that house, but who she was and why she is earthbound at that address remains a mystery.

A Tragic Haunting

One wintry evening in 2009, 57-year-old Rita, a widow, was watching television in her ground-floor flat on Moscow Drive, just off Green Lane (situated between Stoneycroft and Tuebrook) when she thought she heard a scream coming from her kitchen. Rita's ginger-brown cat,

Toffee had been curled up in front of the gas fire on the rug having a doze, but now he was now looking towards the door with wide eyes, because he too had heard the scream. Rita turned down the volume on her television with the remote, then opened the living room door and stepped into the cold hallway. She could hear a child's hysterical cries and what sounded like two frantic women saying things like, 'Oh! Oh no!'

These inexplicable noises were coming from the kitchen. Rita crept to the kitchen door, which was closed, and listened. She could definitely hear frenzied voices, maybe someone had broken into the house via the kitchen window in the backyard, and the widow decided to open the door to confront whoever it was.

As Rita turned the handle and pushed the door wide open, she found only the kitchen in darkness, but a child's high-pitched voice screamed: 'Mummy! Take it out!'

Rita's hand fumbled for the light switch. The neon strip of light in the ceiling flickered on and off a few times, and during the first flicker of neon light, the widow was startled to see a little boy standing in the centre of the kitchen's chequerboard tiles, his little hands on his face, with his fingers at his eyes – as if he was crying. And he had a huge carving knife embedded in his chest, and on the second flicker of the neon light, before it finally came on, Rita caught a glimpse of a huge bloodstain in the boy's shirt. But when the neon light came fully on, the boy was nowhere to be seen.

Rita stood there, gazing at the spot where the boy had stood with the huge knife sticking out of his chest, then backed out of the kitchen, closed the door, and went to get her cat transporter box from under the stairs. She placed a complaining Toffee in the box; he probably associated it with all the times he had been taken to the vet's. Rita turned off the television, grabbed her coat, keys and purse, and walked to her youngest sister's home near Sandfield Park. Rita's sister, Roey (short for Rosemarie), had just finished doing the ironing when she received the surprise visit, and asked what the matter was. Rita, knowing how belittling and sarcastic Roey's husband George was at the best of times, asked Roey in a whisper at the front door if she could talk to her in private. Roey ushered her sister and the cat into the kitchen as George sat in the living room with his feet up on the coffee table, watching the usual soap operas.

Rita told her sister exactly what she had seen, and Roey had no reason to doubt her. Her oldest sister had always been an honest straight-talking person, and Roey had not once heard Rita talk about ghosts or the supernatural.

'What do you think it's been?' Roey asked, picking up Toffee as he was released from his plastic prison.

'A ghost!' Rita replied flatly, and her eyes showed traces of fear. 'It was horrible.'

'A knife in him?' Roey pictured the horrific scene.

Sipping a strong cup of coffee, Rita nodded and with a shudder remembered the screams. 'It sounded as if there were two women with the poor little thing, and one of them was shouting: "Oh! Oh!" and the other woman sounded as if she was panicking as well, but I couldn't quite make out what she was saying.'

'Have you ever seen anything like this before in that house?' Roey asked her.

'No,' said Rita. 'Never seen anything like it, not in that house. Now and then me and me Mam used to hear a woman singing in our old house on Oaky [Oakhill Road], when you were just a toddler, but nothing like this.'

The door flew open and Toffee hissed at George as he leaped into the room. 'Did I scare ya?' he said, with a big grin on his face. He'd been listening at the door.

Roey swore at him and called him an idiot, and George smirked as he went to the freezer to get a bottle of Stella. 'Ghosts! Get Derek Acorah round there and he might get possessed ...' George was saying, when Roey interrupted him with growing fury in her eyes.

'My sister has just had a shock, and I know she's seen something, and you want to grow up. How old are you now, George?' Roey snarled, then turning to an embarrassed Rita, said, 'He hates me reminding him of his age.'

'Oh shut up, you little nag,' George said, and as he walked from the fridge, he gave his wife the middle finger gesture without even turning round.

'Half a century old!' Roey shouted, 'The big five-o and still acting like a teenager!'

George halted, looked at the bottle in his hand, then looked at the wall, as if he was thinking about smashing the Stella against it. He slowly turned round and said: 'Look, let's not get personal, okay? I think ghosts and all that shit are just nonsense.'

Rita raised an eyebrow.

'No disrespect to you Rita ...' George half-apologised.

'No one's interested in what you think, George,' Roey told him as she looked him up and down with a very condescending smile, 'but I happen to believe my sister.'

'Oh, I'm going,' Rita sighed, and she crouched down to pick up Toffee.

'No, don't go, Reet,' Roey said, grabbing her sister's forearm.

'I'll go back with you, Rita,' George suddenly volunteered, realising he'd been too confrontational.

'No, I'll be alright on my own, thanks,' Rita replied, putting Toffee back in his transporter.

But George insisted he'd take Rita home, and he drove her and his wife to the flat on Moscow Drive, and by now the wintry weather had slicked the roads with black ice.

George went into Rita's kitchen first and looked around, and then Rita and her sister came in. Rita pointed to the spot where the boy had stood and Roey felt goosebumps rise on her arms at that spot.

The three of them sat down for about half an hour, and chatted, until George looked bored. He went to the toilet, and when he came back he had blood on his hands. The sisters stopped chatting, and George, examining the red sticky liquid, said: 'Where the hell did that come from?'

Roey trembled and Rita stood up and walked into the hallway. Blood was smeared on the handle of the toilet door.

George sniffed his hand, and remarked: 'Yeah, it's definitely blood. God, where did it come from?'

'Have you cut yourself, love?' Roey asked, walking slowly towards her shocked husband. She had never seen his face this serious.

Rita pushed open the door to the toilet, and saw spots of blood on the floor, and also smeared on the handle on the other side of the door. She gathered some rolls of toilet paper and passed it to George, but the blood was sticky so he went to the wash basin and ran the taps and put his besmeared hands under them. He had grabbed the bar of soap from a dish and had begun to apply it to his palms, when he suddenly cried out.

Rita and Roey ran into the toilet and almost collided with George as he rushed out. He swore loudly and said he had seen a little boy reflected in the mirror, and his little white shirt and light brown trousers were soaked in blood, and his face was contorted and twisted as if he was in agony.

As George was telling the sisters what he had just seen, Rita gasped and wordlessly pointed to something at the end of the dark hallway. Roey and George turned to see what Rita was pointing at.

The flat was, of course, on the ground floor, but in the past this flat of Rita's had formed the downstairs rooms of a house, and a stairway had existed in the hallway that gave access to the upper floors. That stairway had now reappeared and creeping down the stairs was a man dressed all in black, with a face so white and eyes so dark, he was almost clown-like. In this weird stranger's hand he held a long carving knife, and as he slowly descended the stairs with one pale hand on the rail, Rita, Roey and George made a dash for the front door – leaving poor Toffee alone in the house.

The terrified trio waited by the car on Moscow Drive for what seemed like hours, and in the end, Rita, tormented by the thought of Toffee being stabbed by the weird maniac, decided – despite the hysterical protestations of her younger sister – to rush back inside.

When Rita entered her flat, she became very disoriented, because the entire interior had obviously reverted back to the way it had looked a long time ago. The heavy dark curtains, the violet intricately patterned wallpaper, the open blazing fire, and all of the antique furniture and gas bracket fittings looked so uncanny. But not a soul was to be seen. Toffee came meowing from under a table, and Rita scooped him up and dashed out of the house. On the doorstep, she saw George wrestling with his wife, preventing her from going into the house. When they saw Rita coming out they went with her to the car, and Rita could hardly get her words out. 'Go to yours,' she said to George, and he started the vehicle then stalled it with nerves. He restarted the car and accelerated off up Moscow Drive, headed for Green Lane.

Rita, Roey and George and the couple's teenaged daughter Melanie, went back to the haunted flat on Moscow Drive that night and found the front door still open. Now the flat's interior had returned to normal, but enough was enough, but Rita could not bear the possibility of further supernatural disturbances and she and her cat later moved to a flat many miles away in Aigburth Vale.

I have scoured the records and archives and to date, I cannot explain the reasons for the haunting of the flat on Moscow Drive. Perhaps a child was murdered there, and the murder never came to light, and perhaps on the anniversary of the despicable crime, some ghastly re-enactment takes place. There are a few haunted residences on Moscow Drive, but they are tame in comparison with the haunting which forced a woman to flee from her home and converted her sceptical brother-in-law into a believer in the strange ways of the supernatural.

SOME HALLOWEEN TALES

As you are reading this book, and have some interest in the supernatural, it's likely that you're fond of Halloween, a time we traditionally associate with ghosts, ghouls, vampires and, of course, witches, and Liverpool and Wirral have been the scene of some spectacular witchery over the years, from Jenny Green, Arch Witch of St James's Mount, where the Anglican Cathedral now stands, to the Molloy Coven of Liverpool's eighteenth century Castle Street, right through to the Pendle Witch trials, and the antics of Mary O'Lohan – the Bootle Witch. Who? You may ask, well she's one of this region's less well known witches. I once met Layla, a descendant of this witch at a book-signing several years ago, and found the young redheaded teenager's face tantalisingly familiar. I enquired about her surname and the girl's answer astounded me. It was an unmistakable surname which meant she was a descendant of the Bootle Witch. Layla looked just like the etching of Mary O'Lohan, who originally hailed from Western Eire in the early nineteenth century. As I tried to find the pen I'd mislaid, I told Layla the following little story, cobbled together from research into the Bootle Witch over a few years.

In the 1870s, four robbers from Wallasey set out in a rowing boat on the night of 31 October – All Hallow's Eve, and under the cover of darkness they came ashore at Bootle. The hardened criminals prowled the sandhills and soon spotted a solitary oil lamp burning in the window of a cottage which they subsequently broke into. An old and rather diminutive hunch-backed woman lived alone there, and offered little resistance to the seaborne thugs, who stole all of her valuables, including a mahogany chest, which they could not open. The tiny old lady pointed at one of the cowardly robbers and uttered a strange phrase, and he suddenly found he could hardly see; everything looked blurred. Realising the woman was some kind of witch, one of the robbers pushed her into the fire, then they all went back to the shore, stifling laughter and sniggering about the easiest job they'd carried out in a while. The four men set out on to the calm waters, but after a few minutes of frantic rowing, a storm whipped up, and searing forks of lightning flashed across Liverpool Bay. 'It's witchery! That crone has called up Neptune!' said the thugs' leader, but one of his lackeys hypocritically made the sign of the cross and said, 'Lord protect us.'

All of a sudden, an enormous black shadowy mass rose up out of the sea – and formed the image of a beautiful red-haired woman with outstretched arms, visible from the waist upwards. The sea rose up and waves capsized the boat as screeching female laughter ripped through the howling air. Three of the robbers drowned, but the leader, Bill Purvis, survived, although he became permanently impotent and lost all of his hair soon afterwards.

It was said that many years later at a Liverpool market, Bill saw the very same red-haired woman whose apparition had appeared that terrifying night over the capsized boat. He learnt from his enquiries, that it was Mary O'Lohan – a real-life witch from Bootle. It had been her grandmother that Bill and his men had robbed and injured that night. Bill Purvis is said to have attempted to burn Mary O'Lohan's cottage one evening, but the sands of the beautiful beach that once graced unspoilt Bootle's shores, seemed to open up and he was sucked beneath the sands into choking oblivion.

Layla loved this little dark piece of her 'family history' but still I couldn't find my pen to sign her book – when suddenly, an old Waterman fountain pen seemed to appear out of nowhere next to my hand on the table. I signed Layla's book with the quaint pen, looked away for a moment, then realised the descendant of the Bootle Witch had gone – along with that vintage pen ...

Witches are still around today, of course, and the only people who hunt them nowadays are eager students of Wicca who long to become witches themselves, but most are witches by birth, and few are made, or are the results of some correspondence course. A listener to the *Billy Butler Show* once contacted me on air to ask if I had ever heard about a man who levitated in front of quite a few witnesses on Hope Street in the Sixties. Radio is a powerful tool for connecting people and the million-plus listeners to my slot are often more productive than any search engine. Within minutes of the caller's enquiry about the levitating man, telephone calls were made to the station and I was able to talk to a man who claimed he was the one who had been lifted into the air that autumnal day in 1965. He told me a very bizarre story in an effort to throw some light on the gravity-defying incident.

On Saturday, 30 October 1965, at 5pm, 24-year-old coalman Carl Woodbridge sat at the family table at his terraced home in Kensington watching the television whilst eating his tea. He loved Saturdays like this. The *Sports Result Service* was on the box, and as Carl ate his tea, he scoured the television guide: *Robin Hood* was on in a minute, then *Thank Your Lucky Stars*, followed by *Thunderbirds*, *The*

Big Valley, and Charlie Drake in *The Worker*. Tomorrow would be even better, when Carl would take his new girlfriend Carol Tillyabot to the Cavern to see The Who, the Aztecs and the Big Three. But out of the blue, something bizarre happened that Saturday afternoon.

Carl suddenly lost his appetite, and for some reason he began to think of a girl he had seen on his rounds as a coalman on Huskisson Street. She was about 19, red-haired, with a shapely figure and an elfin-like face. It struck the young coalman as being rather bizarre that the girl's face should suddenly come into his mind. With butterflies in his stomach, Carl got up from the table, grabbed his coat, and ignored his mother when she asked him why he had left his food and where he was going. Walking almost trance-like down the hallway, Carl took the bunch of flowers (purchased from Fishlock's the Florists of Elliot Street) from the cool larder's slate shelf, and walked out of the house to the bus stop.

'What's got into you?' Mrs Woodbridge yelled after him, and Carl thought: 'I wish I knew, Mam.'

He got as far as Hope Street, within a few yards of the corner of Huskisson Street, when the face of his girlfriend Carol came into his mind. One half of his heart yearned for the beautiful redhead and the other half still belonged to Carol. It was a strange agony, and Carl felt like an indecisive donkey between two piles of strawberries, unable to choose which way to turn. The seductive face of the stunning redhead appeared clearly in his mind's eye – and he could see every freckle and every fair eyelash. His heart pounded with lust, but then all of a sudden, Carl felt something curl around his body like a giant boa constrictor, and it lifted him high into the air! It was as if a giant hand was holding him aloft, and this act of levitation was witnessed by many startled passers-by. The 'hand' deposited Carl about 12 feet away from the point of his vertical departure, and he was so shaken by the weird experience of momentary weightlessness, he forgot all about the redhead and went home.

On the following day, just before he was to set out for the Cavern with Carol, he told her what had happened, expecting her to disbelieve him and to be a bit peeved at his unaccountable fixation with the redhead, but Carol told him something that he couldn't take in at first. 'I picked you up,' she said, and smiled.

Carl just laughed.

Carol giggled and nodded. 'Yes, that was me,' she said in a reassuring tone. Then she claimed that she was a witch, and told Carl his 'sudden obsession' with the redhead had in fact been a powerful spell the redhead had put on him, as she too fancied him.

'Oh, she's a witch too?' Carl laughed, thinking, hoping, that it was all some joke with a punchline to come. But Carol replied, 'Yes ... she's my sister. She always tries to steal my boyfriends.'

And it was true, the redhead was indeed Carol's sister, Isabel Tillyabot. It took some time for Carl to get his head round the situation, but he later married Carol anyway, and when I spoke to him, he was a happily married man in his sixties. He did tell me that his grandchildren had inherited Carol's 'talent'.

My own sister was a practising witch in her teenage years, and I believe it was her amateur spell-casting and rituals that probably stirred up so many of the ghosts in our old home. She was especially active at Halloween, one of the ancient fire festivals of the Druids, when the invisible world of the supernatural is at its closest to this world, according to the occultists of long ago. Halloween night is the one night of the year when everyday mortals can supposedly look into the future and find answers by paranormal means, and most of these methods of divination involve mirrors.

There was a case, reported to me many years ago, in the 1970s, of a teenager named Claire, who had a strange dream involving a mirror; a dream which revealed a shocking secret.

The story begins in Kirkby in October 1975. Claire had just turned eighteen that month, and for three solid weeks, starting on around the 1st or 2nd of October, her mother Edna had been having an incredible run of bad luck. It began when a front tooth suddenly became loose one day at teatime and fell out. Then she suffered a heavy nosebleed whilst driving and crashed her car into a bus stop (luckily there was no one waiting for a bus at the time). An irritating rash broke out under Edna's breasts, and anti-fungal creams and all manner of lotions couldn't soothe it. Indeed, the rash then spread down her arms. Not long after this, agonising headaches began to plague the mother of three to such an extent, she had to stay off work for a few days. At this time Edna was working at the local Bird's Eye factory, and her work attendance record up to this time had been excellent. Even when Edna had a cold she would go into work as she actually found her job bearable.

Around this time, Claire's beautiful friend, Isla Coventry, was staying over with her at the house in Northwood, and Isla kindly tried to nurse Edna back to health, bringing soup and countless cups of tea and hot toddies up to Claire's ailing mum, whilst Claire seemed more concerned with a local lad named Jeff (who did not seem at all interested in her) than her mother's condition. Edna's husband, Gerry, suspected that all of the maladies supposedly affecting his wife were imaginary, and there was a blazing row between the couple when she overheard an insensitive remark of his downstairs in the kitchen one morning. 'All this palaver for Bette Davis. Acting the goat at her age,' he had moaned to Isla as the girl was stirring a pan of chicken soup for Edna on the stove.

The doctor came out and Edna said she felt as if someone was stabbing her in her belly during the night. The doctor used a stethoscope to listen to her abdomen and diagnosed a gastric condition which would clear itself up after a period of rest. He advised Edna to eat bland food for a few days. The headaches were the result of nerves, brought on by a lack of sleep, the doctor opined, and then left.

Isla ironed Gerry's shirts and trousers, and even made breakfast for the family, and Gerry and his two sons were really appreciative of the girl's altruism, and before Gerry went to work one morning he said to Claire: 'Why can't you be more like Isla and do breakfast and a bit or ironing now and then, eh? You're a lazy sod, you know.'

That same morning, Edna's weak voice floated down the stairs, crying out for Claire. Isla went up to see what the matter was, but Edna told the girl: 'You've done enough, love; can you tell Claire to come up and see me please?'

Claire stomped up the stairs to see her mum. She had been browsing through a catalogue to find a black leather coat to impress Jeff, as she'd heard he liked girls in leather. 'What?' Claire almost snapped upon entering her parents' bedroom. Edna looked terrible: dark rings round her heavy eyes, and a pale, almost jaundiced pallor to her complexion. 'Claire, give your Nan this letter,' she said, and she made a great effort to prop herself up and took a small pale blue envelope from under the pillows.

'What?' Claire asked, dreading the thought of leaving the house to go on an errand in the cold October air. 'Which Nan do you mean? Me Dad's mam or ...'

'Nanny Sue, my mother,' Edna replied, and her chest sounded wheezy. 'Go now please, girl, it's important.'

'Mam, I was just looking through the catalogue for a coat; that's important too ...' Claire seemed ready to explode into one of her usual tantrums.

Edna knew her daughter had a crush on Jeff, and she recalled that he lived in the same area as Nanny Sue. 'Your Nan lives in Southdene, do you remember where her house is? It's by that Jeff fellah's house at the end of Bewley Drive.'

There was a pause as a slight smile formed on Claire's lips. Her big eyes widened at the mention of Jeff. 'I can't go like this,' and Claire looked down at her old sweater and jeans. 'I'll have to put some decent clothes on ... for me Nanna.' Claire snatched the envelope and went to get changed. She returned to the bedroom 40 minutes later with plucked eyebrows and a face coated in foundation, dressed more for a night out than for a flying visit to Nanny Sue's, but Edna understood why and said nothing.

Isla stayed to look after Edna as Claire tottered off in her high heeled boots down Old Rough Lane through a freezing knife-edged wind. Nanny Sue opened the letter and her eyes seemed to dance about through the lenses of her specs as she read the message from Edna. Claire, meanwhile, was at the window, hoping to catch a glimpse of the incredibly handsome Jeff pass by.

'Your mother thinks someone has cursed her,' Sue said, squinting at the note. 'The Evil Eye has been cast on her, she thinks ... Claire?'

'What?' Claire turned her face from the net curtains. 'The what Eye?'

'Someone has cursed your mother from the looks of it. All these things happening to her go far beyond the law of averages, girl. But who would want to put such a nasty spell on her?' Sue told her grandaughter, and she beckoned her to a small dark room upstairs. The place was full of old books, and a crystal ball rested on a table, half covered with a black velvet cloth. The old woman rummaged through a drawer and then she handed Claire a small brown paper bag crammed with tiny white flowers. 'Tell your mother to put this under her pillow and she'll dream of the person who put the Evil Eye on her. It's a herb called yarrow. Girls used to see who they would marry if they put this under their pillows on Duck Apple Night ... Halloween.'

This claim really captured Claire's imagination, and as it was Halloween, the girl used a bit of the yarrow she'd taken from the brown bag, and placed it under her pillow. Edna dreamed of nothing, possibly because she was so ill and run-down, but Claire had the strangest yet most realistic dream. She was looking in a mirror, and a red glowing man, who she took to be a demon of some sort, announced, 'Jeff does not love you and never will lust for any woman.' And then the crimson-skinned entity declared: 'Here is the witch who is out to kill your mother, for she loves your father!' And Isla appeared in the mirror!

When Claire awoke, she sneaked past the door to the spare bedroom where Isla was sleeping, and informed her mum of the revelatory dream. 'I knew it! I knew it; she's been too helpful. Couldn't do enough for me!'

Edna recalled what her mother used to say about tackling witches: they cannot stand accusation. If you accuse them of being a witch in front of people, they lose their powers for a while and usually flee – and this is exactly what happened on the following day at breakfast. Edna was so ill she almost crawled downstairs, and in front of her husband, Claire, and her three older sons, she denounced Isla saying, 'I accuse you of being a witch, Isla!'

Gerry smirked for a moment at his wife's bizarre outburst, then quipped: 'What are you on about?' He presumed her illness had made her delirious.

Isla fled from the table and ran out of the house without a word of reply. With Isla out of the way, Edna soon made a full recovery, and she and her mother fixed old iron horseshoes over the back and front doors of the house, as iron traditionally repels witches. It later came to light that Gerry had been having an affair with Isla during her stay-overs at the house, something that was so out of character for him. Perhaps he had literally been spellbound. Gerry begged Edna to forgive him, and swore he did not even know why he had slept with the teenaged girl, and Edna, who had been with her husband long enough to know when he was telling the truth, forgave him.

Isla kept herself scarce and eventually moved away to another area, and Jeff – as the demon in the mirror forecast – never did 'lust for any woman', because he was gay, and proudly announced it to the world when rumours began to spread about his sexuality.

Isla belonged to a certain Kirkby coven that is alleged to have held sabbats in the churchyard of St Chad's. A teacher once told me how a five-year-old girl from this family of witches once saw a picture of an old fashioned broom in a book, and remarked: 'That's Nanna's horse!' The child then told the intrigued teacher how her grandmother 'rode' the broom and even flew about.

There is something about Halloween that goes beyond the light-hearted rituals of Duck Apple Night and trick or treat. I've spent so much of my life investigating the supernatural, and I have noticed that some of the strangest, most inexplicable incidents seem to occur at the beginning of October and peak around the end of the month. Perhaps the originators of Halloween, the Celts, and other ancient peoples of this country, were more conscious of this period of strangeness than folk today, because they were living closer to nature, whereas most of us are becoming couch zombies, anaesthetised by mind-numbing television shows and adverts, inane internet content and a needless urge to have the latest mobile or technological gadget.

In times past, the 'Eating the Apple at the Glass' scrying ritual took place on Halloween, and supposedly enabled participants to glimpse their future husband or wife. You light a candle before a mirror at midnight, and cut an apple into small pieces as you stand at least 12 feet from the looking glass. Have a comb or brush on you. You throw a piece of the apple over your left shoulder then eat the pieces of apple as you approach the mirror, simultaneously combing or brushing your hair downwards. Stand for a while gazing at the mirror and the face of the one you'll marry will appear over your left shoulder in your reflection.

One Halloween evening in Woolton in 1972, 28-year-old Sam settled down with a cuppa to watch a new situation comedy on BBC 1 called *My Wife Next Door*, about a couple in the throes of a messy divorce who each buy a cottage in the country, only to find the cottages are adjacent to each other. As Sam watched the comedy, she saw the scene change to show what was unmistakably the back of her husband's head – and he was passionately kissing another woman, a redhead. Sam gasped in disbelief and then the heads faded away and the comedy programme came back on. This was at 8.40pm. Sam obviously couldn't enjoy the rest of the programme and so she switched it off and sat there baffled. That colour television had come into her possession when her grandmother died; could that have some bearing on the spooky incident? Sam's grandmother used to say no man could be trusted.

That night her husband Don came back from a supposed visit to a friend's house at 11pm, and before Sam could say a word about the 'vision', he suddenly broke down and admitted he had almost started an affair with his secretary earlier in the evening, but had quickly come to his senses 'after just one kiss'. Sam then stunned him when she asked: 'Was she a redhead?'

Don didn't believe Sam's version about the phantom scene on the television; he thought she'd actually got someone to spy on him, but she eventually convinced him that through some supernatural means, she had somehow seen him and the secretary as they kissed in the latter's Wirral home at Bidston Avenue.

On the following Halloween, just after teatime, Sam and Don

were watching television when they suddenly witnessed a car crash in the middle of a weather forecast. The disturbing excerpt must have flashed for only about three seconds, but Don was able to say that the car had been driving on the wrong side of the road. After the last episode they wondered if this was an omen, and dreaded news of a car crash. Sure enough, later that night, Don's sister telephoned him to say that her husband had been killed in a car crash in France. Don immediately recalled that the car he and Sam had seen crashing on the television screen had been driving on the right side of the road – just as motorists do in France.

A few days after this creepy occurrence, Sam saw a picture of a man's face, covered in blood, on the television screen. The man looked as if he was screaming but no sound accompanied the distressing picture. Sam and Don expected a call of some other tragedy after the latest ominous vision on the colour television but, thankfully, they never received any bad news and so never discovered the identity of the man with the blood-drenched face.

When Sam was out of the house one day, Don gave the television set to Oxfam because he was so scared of what it might reveal in the future.

THE MUGGER ON LARK LANE

I am fascinated by unusual surnames, and therefore clearly recall the second name of Glen Ipsintaut. One bitterly cold December night in 2010, Glen was at a certain public house in the south end of Liverpool, wallowing in what he perceived to be his failure of a life. His 40-year-old wife Lucy had recently had an hysterectomy because of a rare condition of the womb, and while she recovered at their home in Aigburth, he gloomily bemoaned the fact that they could never have children. The couple had been too busy to have kids when they were in their thirties, and now they'd lost their chance of ever having any, and Glen didn't want to adopt either.

'None to make you laugh, and none to make you cry,' the landlord said, and tried to change the subject by droning on about the specific gravity of his beer, but Glen Ipsintaut was lost in a world of self-pity, and the vodkas and tonics were only making his glum outlook even worse, because all alcohol is a depressive. 'There's got to be more to life than this,' Glen told his reflection in the mirror that was engraved with the word 'Schweppes' set out in an arch. The time was coming up to one in the morning, and there were now only seven people – including the landlord – left in the parlour. The lock-ins at this pub had been getting seriously rare over the past year; perhaps because of the mini recessions, or the cheap booze at the off licences, or perhaps people were simply fed up of the old pub's environment.

'There's always someone worse off than you,' said an old man leaning against the counter, about three feet to the right of Glen. He turned to face a miserable old man. He had obviously been listening to Glen's grumbles all night. 'Tomorrow's another day,' the old man said, 'just go home and sleep on it.'

'What for?' Glen said to the pensioner as he headed for the door. 'It'll only be the same thing tomorrow and the day after that.'

'Night, George,' the landlord said to the departing old man and then went to the door to bolt it after him. Just before he fastened the door, old George zipped up his coat and craned back his head to survey the full moon. 'He's very bright tonight,' he mused, then walked off down the snow-covered street.

The landlord gently closed the door and slid the bolt.

The old clock on the wall suddenly emitted a single chime as it reached one o'clock, which startled the landlord. 'That clock hasn't chimed for years ... how odd,' he said, thinning his eyes at the ivory face of the Tiffany & Co timepiece, which was bought in New York by a previous landlord in the 1950s.

'I think I'll be getting home,' said Glen, half-heartedly eyeing the temperamental wall clock, and grabbed his mackintosh which had been hanging over a barstool. At the door, as the stinging cold night air touched Glen's face, the landlord said, 'Tell Lucy I was asking about her,' and Glen nodded glumly and walked out into the street. The snow, which was hardening with the sub-zero temperatures, crunched under Glen's feet. For some subconscious reason, he decided to go home via the streets that had once formed part of his old neighbourhood, and it never entered Glen's head that Lucy would be worried sick if he was home later than 1am. He'd switched off his mobile because he didn't want anyone disturbing his mood at the moment. The sky was cloudless, and the full moon's light was glistening off the ivory rooftops and the glossy icing of the roads and pavements. The rhythmic scrunching of Glen's soles on the icy snow layer seemed muffled to him, as if the snow, which covered everything, had affected the acoustics of the world and dampened every noise, producing an eerie dreamlike silence which hung in the air. Then Glen smelt a scent of a tobacco brand that sent him back years: Drum. It was close by, and getting stronger, and Glen turned a corner and almost collided with a shabbily-dressed man.

Glen bowed his head and walked on, realising it had been a mistake to go home via memory lane. The man behind him, automatically regarded as a 'no mark' in Glen's mode of thinking, probably had a knife or even a gun if the stories in the newspapers were anything to go by nowadays, but how could someone who had had a bit too much to drink make a quick getaway on these skating rink pavements? Come winter, Glen would always curse the sluggish council for never having enough grit for any snowfall.

'Hey, I know you!' came a voice through the dead muffled air, but Glen didn't look back at the scally. He used his old trick of reaching into his inside pocket as he crossed the road, hoping the shady nonentity would think he had a gun. It didn't work. Glen glanced to his right and saw the pathetic scruff hurrying after him. He was bald with dark greasy strands of hair on each side of his head, and a cigarette dangled from his mouth – a roll-up by the smell of it. He wore a green stained padded coat, jeans creased like a concertina, and a pair of scuffed non-brand trainers on his feet.

'Hey, I know you,' he repeated, and after a pause, added. 'Don't you know me?'

'Piss off or I'll call the police!' And Glen took his mobile out of his inside coat pocket. He turned it on but it seemed to take much longer than usual to log on to the network. He looked round – not a soul, and not a taxi to be seen anywhere. In the old days he could have taken a short cut down an entry but people like the specimen of lowlife trailing behind him had caused the council to put alleygates across the entries to stop burglars using them to gain back door access to their jobs. It was the same with the roads; speed bumps everywhere because of mindless joyriders and speeding car thieves. Glen lifted the phone to his face and said, 'Police please,' even though he was not speaking to anyone. It was all bluff because of he was desperate.

'What are you calling the police for? I haven't done anything wrong!' the seedy stranger moaned as he stopped and took the roll-up from his mouth.

'A man's trying to mug me ...' Glen told the make-believe police operator.

'I'm not!' protested the man, flinging his roll-up stub down into the snow with anger.

'Yes, he's armed ... he has a knife ...'

'Lying bastard!'

'I'm at the Aigburth Road end of Lark Lane, please hurry!'

And Glen turned to his potential mugger, hoping he'd now run off, but he stood his ground, and seemed to be crying. 'Don't you know who I am yet?' he asked. 'Don't you recognise me?'

Glen's stomach went into freefall as he suddenly realised what the undesirable was trying to make him see. His body went numb and dizzy from the revelation. He was looking at himself. Glen wore a small hairpiece, and when he took it off each night, he saw the face that was looking at him now in the bathroom mirror. The 'mugger' was in need of a shave and a good night's sleep by the looks of it, and possibly had a drug problem.

Many years ago when Glen had lived in this area he had smoked Drum tobacco. He had suffered from acute insomnia during those lonely years when he could find no partner and no employment prospects. His face was as pallid as the loser before him. No holidays, no tanning sessions in those days, and no dress sense or any inclination of what was fashionable before he met Lucy, who had turned his life around. She had given him confidence and a sense of pride and direction. Glen felt as if he was looking at a version of himself who had never met Lucy, but he wasn't sure whether it was the vodka playing tricks on his depressed mind, or whether this no-hoper standing before him merely bore an uncanny resemblance – but if this was so, why had he asked, 'Don't you know who I am yet?'

'Are you real or is this some crazy dream?' the look-alike asked Glen, and he mopped tears away with the sleeve of his coat.

'Is your name Glen, too?' Glen asked with a cough, because his throat closing up through fear.

The bald man nodded. 'I could have been you, couldn't I?' he asked, and now the tears were really streaming from his eyes.

Glen turned and he ran, and he had put about 30 feet between himself and the doppelganger when he slipped and fell heavily in the snow. The less successful Glen – the one who saw himself as a failure – went to his aid, but was angrily kicked away. Glen swore at his 'inferior copy' and then ran on again, but fell skidded and fell. This time the non-starter stayed put, and merely watched as Glen crawled away on all fours, getting up, falling down, until he found he was alone.

When he reached home, Glen's red-raw hands trembled as he searched his pockets for his house keys. He went into his warm home and sat in the kitchen, shaking as he went over every word he and the eerie double had exchanged, then headed straight to the drinks cabinet in the lounge. There was only a small drop of brandy in a bottle and Glen drained it into his mouth. He then went to the bathroom, bathed his face in warm water, and then undressed and went to bed, where Lucy was lying face down, fast asleep.

Before Glen embraced her, he went to his window and noted that new snow was beginning to fall. Through the blinds he caught a brief glimpse of *him* – a solitary silhouette of a broken man, passing the end of the street, walking in the white limbo of snow to who knows where. Glen never set eyes on his doppelganger again, and nor did he ever moan again about the way his life had turned out after that chastening encounter. From that day onwards he often wondered if he would have turned out exactly like the hopeless man he had met that wintry night if he had not had the good fortune to meet Lucy.

The Secret of Castle Hill

The Halloween of 1973 fell on a Wednesday, and on that day a brother and sister from West Derby went to stay at the house of their Uncle Jack for a week. The sky was of a deep oceanic blue that first day at Uncle Jack's home when 13-year-old David and his 11-year-old sister Melody went to play in the vast green fields surrounding Castle Hill, a mysterious ancient mound in Newton-le-Willows that has baffled archaeologists and antiquarians for centuries. The children were supposed to be looking after their uncle, who had experienced a mild stroke, but he had insisted on them playing out on such an unusually sunny day for October.

The time was around 2.40pm, and David was flying his cherished Peter Powell stunt kite high over Castle Hill as Melody played with her skipping rope. To David's left, he could see the crescent moon hanging in the sky, even though it was daytime, and as he made the kite hedge hop, he noticed some other white object in the sky to his right. He thought it was a plane at first, but as he squinted skywards, the object was lost in the glare of the low sun. About a minute later, as David's kite was looping the loop, Melody suddenly stopped skipping and hurried over to her brother to tell him something, but David was too engrossed with the kite to pay her any attention, so she tapped his forearm repeatedly.

'What?' David growled, and Melody just pointed up into the sky. David looked up and saw what looked like a man in a white flowing robe and cape, flying through the blue sky – in the direction of the Peter Powell kite. David was lost for words.

'What is it?' Melody asked as David tried to steer the kite away from the surreal-looking sky-borne figure. Melody's sharp vision could discern some sort of white pointed hood on the flying man which later reminded her of the ones worn by members of the Ku Klux Klan in the States, but what really scared her was the long curved sword it was wielding. 'Let's go!' Melody cried, and tugged frantically at the sleeve of her brother's pullover, but David stood his ground, trying to yank the kite away from the flying white-clad figure. 'It's got my kite!' he yelled as the sinister flier man seized the red kite with his right hand. With his other hand he proceeded to slash the sail fabric of the kite with the fearsome-looking sword! As the kite fell to earth in tatters the creepy figure began to swoop down as the wind billowed through his weird garments, and David and Melody ran off as fast as their legs could carry them, all the way home. The kite was later found in shreds on the slopes of the hill.

Uncle Jack believed the children's tale, and said they had seen one of the ancient ghosts who guard the 'burial mound' of Castle Hill, where, legend says, chieftains of thousands of years ago were interred with all sorts of treasure.

Another ghost on Castle Hill is a frequently-reported lady in white who drifts across the nearby M6 motorway causing the occasional crash. The white lady has been seen for at least a century, and was mostly encountered by poachers out after dark in the area around Castle Hill. The hooded male figure in white has been seen flying over Castle Hill and wears a red circle emblem with an unknown symbol in the centre. From that little detail I believe the figure may be a ghostly sentinel who belonged to the 'Lily White Boys', an obscure sect in these parts that pre-dated even the Druids. The Lily White Boys wore pointed hoods with eye-holes, and their chiefs were said to have worn a strange circular emblem on their garments. What's more, the Lily White Boys were said to be able to levitate and run at incredible speeds because they utilised a form of 'telluric' power derived from the earth itself. If recent reports are anything to go by, the white robed monk-like figure and the White Lady are still haunting Castle Hill, and the secret of the ancient mound remains a mystery.

Glasgow Smile

Some years ago I came out of the studios of Radio Merseyside and in the station's reception area was met by a woman in her sixties named Gwenda who had waited for me to come off air after talking about local mysteries on the *Billy Butler Show*. Gwenda asked me if I knew of any ghosts that haunted the Oxford Street area of the city, and I recalled a few. There was a woman in a babushka scarf and a shabby long coat who carried a deceased baby in her arms. She talked with an Irish lilt and was thought to be an emigrant from Ireland who had been murdered near Cambridge Street in Victorian times. The other ghost of note was 'Glasgow Smile' – a prostitute who haunted Arrad Street (at the back of the Everyman Theatre) as well as parts of Hope Street, Mount Pleasant and Oxford Street. Gwenda's eyes widened at the mention of this ghost, and seconds later a tear welled in her eye. I took Gwenda to a cafe on Bold Street where she told me just why she had posed a question about Oxford Street ghosts. In her younger days, Gwenda had been a prostitute herself for a while, and in the November of 1971, her pimp had stationed her on the Oxford Street 'beat'. At this time, Gwenda had just turned 30, and she had lost her mother, father and older brother to cancer within 13 months, and on top of that, her grandmother was admitted to hospital after suffering a severe stroke. Gwenda had no one to turn to, and her pimp took advantage of her insecurity and manipulated her in despicable ways I could never detail in print.

On the first night on Oxford Street, the prospect of finding a client seemed non existent, and Gwenda huddled in a bus shelter, shivering in the November wind coming up from the river. All she wanted to do was go home. She recalled the lovely nights when she would sit with her grandmother all snug in front of the fire and listen to her stories about the old days over a mug of cocoa.

As Gwenda reminisced, a car came crawling down Oxford Street from the direction of Abercromby Square, and the driver stooped down as his vehicle slowed so he could get a good look at Gwenda.

His face radiated menace, and Gwenda was glad when he drove on and turned into Hope Street by the Medical Institute. About 15 minutes later, faint footsteps approached from the darkness of Arrad Street, and Gwenda turned to see a woman of about her own age, dressed like someone out of a 1930s film. On her head was a bell-shaped hat, or cloche, and she wore a knee-length coat trimmed with fur, dark stockings and pointed black shoes. Only then did Gwenda notice her face. There were two lines leading from the sides of her mouth, from the lips, and they curved upwards through the cheeks until they reached the tails of the woman's eyelashes, forming a macabre impression of a smile. The smile wasn't a drawn-on one – it looked like a deep scar etched into her face. The woman's mouth opened impossibly wide and she let out an ear-splitting scream as she charged towards Gwenda, who dashed away up Oxford Street.

It turned out that the 1930s-styled nutter hadn't been attacking Gwenda – her target was actually the kerb-crawler who had driven by earlier and had now returned and was sneaking up on Gwenda as she stood by the bus stop – and this time he had a knife in his hand. He ran off towards Mount Pleasant with the screaming woman in close pursuit, and as Gwenda looked on from the corner of Mulberry Street, she saw the screaming woman vanish. Gwenda then made herself scarce, and realising she had seen a ghost, and had also come within seconds of being knifed, she decided to quit her occupation, no matter how hard up she was.

Gwenda later learned from other prostitutes that she had encountered 'Glasgow Smile' – the troubled ghost of a Scottish prostitute who had been found unconscious near Arrad Street in the late 1920s or early 1930s with her face mutilated. The attacker had carved a smile into the woman's face with his knife, destroying her looks. Unable to work because of her disfiguration, 'Glasgow' committed suicide by jumping into the Mersey. Not long afterwards though, the ghost of the prostitute was seen roaming the streets of her old beat, and she was even known to protect some women on the game from violent clients.

As late as October 2007, two female students bumped into

Glasgow Smile on Mount Pleasant as they walked home from the Cavern club to their digs off Mulberry Street. The time was about 2.20am, and the students, Natasha and Ella, noticed they were being followed as they walked past the John Foster Building on Mount Pleasant. Ella was the one who first noticed that the woman walking silently behind them was dressed in a purplish coat and the out-of-date cloche hat, but Natasha was the one who saw the grotesque incised smile on the ghost's chalk-white face, and at first Natasha thought the woman was wearing a Halloween mask or 'horror make-up' as Halloween was only a week away. Perhaps the woman had been to some Halloween-themed party. But then as the students reached the Oxford Street branch of Lloyds, Ella decided to withdraw some money at the ATM, and as she did so the girls looked back – and saw something chilling. The woman in the old-fashioned clothes was now on the other side of Oxford Street, and yet seconds ago she had been about 20 feet away. Ella was keying in her PIN number when suddenly the woman appeared next to her, before vanishing into thin air. Ella grabbed her money and she and Natasha clung to one another as they ran home, terrified that they would meet the woman again round every corner.

I must just add this final tale before we leave Glasgow Smile, for it concerns another prostitute, and once more the story touches on the supernatural, only on this occasion it does not involve a ghost.

In 1966, 25-year-old prostitute Christine picked up a client one night at around half-past eleven by the Jacaranda club on Slater Street in the city centre. The client was only about 20 years of age, dressed immaculately in a finely-cut suit, and he had a refined educated voice. This punter was led by Christine into a dark alleyway off Seel Street, where she frequently took her clients. They had barely left the main thoroughfare when the young man suddenly began to kiss her face all over then sank his teeth into her neck. The pain was so excruciating Christine almost passed out. The punter was able to suck quite a quantity of blood from the prostitute's neck, before she somehow managed to let out an ear-piercing scream which summoned several men who had been passing by.

Having thrown Christine to the ground, the man then ran towards a wall which formed the backyard of a derelict house – and leapt to the top of it in one bound. This wall was about 12 feet high. Christine's neck wound looked so serious, she was admitted to the Royal Infirmary on Pembroke Place – where a doctor told her that her attacker must have possessed very long pointed canines to have inflicted such a wound. Christine was given a tetanus jab, and when she returned to her home on Russell Street, she was so weak, her mother and brother had to carry her to bed.

From that night onwards, Christine had nightmares about the 'vampire', and sometimes woke believing he had somehow gained access to her room during the night.

Some three months after this strange incident, another prostitute, 50-year-old Ruth, from Everton, was attacked by a young client in the shadows of a warehouse in the Islington area of the city, and this client bit so deep and long into Ruth's neck, and sucked out such a quantity of blood, she was left lying on the ground in shock. On this occasion, no one witnessed the attack or saw if the attacker had fled the scene in the dramatic fashion of the previous attacker. Ruth was taken to the Royal Infirmary, and when a doctor examined the awful neck wounds, he remarked that this was the third attack he had seen on women in the past few weeks, suggesting that one person was responsible for all three. Just who the vampiric assailant was remains unknown.

THE LAD IN THE HALLWAY

The following spooky story was told to me by the daughter of the woman featured in the account. One wintry morning in the mid-1960s, at around 3.30am, 69-year-old widow, Joan Chapell-Simons, was startled out of her sleep by a faint bang. Joan wasn't sure if she had dreamt the noise or whether it was real, but once she was awake, she found it hard to get back to sleep, and feeling the urge to go the toilet, she left the cosy warmth of her bed and switched on her bedside lamp. The room was swimming with floaters – dead cells within the vitreous humour of Joan's tired eyes. She went into the hallway, but didn't switch on the light there, because the light from the toilet had been left on, as it always was throughout the night, and the faint luminance shining from under the toilet door as a glowing horizontal strip lit up the end of the hallway – and that light also revealed something very alarming indeed: a young man who looked to be about 17 or 18 years of age was crouched on the floor, just a couple of feet from the front door.

Joan immediately assumed, as most of us would, that her home had been broken into by a burglar. She lived on Brodie Avenue in West Allerton, a rather up-market area of the city where burglaries were relatively rare in those days. She froze, then walked backwards a few steps to reach out for the hallway light switch. She clicked it on and now she could clearly see that the burglar was hunkering down on the floor with a look of terror on his face. He wore a white shirt, dark trousers and black shiny shoes.

'Get out of here before I call the police!' Joan yelled, trying to put conviction in her voice.

The youth looked just as afraid as the widow, and put his arm up to shield him from the light that had just come on. He suddenly grabbed his own head with his hands and screwed his face up as if he was in great agony. 'My head! Oh, my head!'

'Help!' Joan shouted, and she ran into the bedroom, closed the door, and leaned against it as she surveyed the dimly-lit room, searching for a weapon. She saw the Rookwood vase, rumoured to be worth hundreds of pounds, standing on the dresser, but decided not to throw it at the young burglar. There had to be another object she could use as a missile.

Then came a heavy knocking at the front door.

Joan felt quite faint now, for she imagined that an accomplice was at the door, but then she heard the knock again, and this time a voice cried out: 'Police!'

Joan opened her bedroom window and saw a police car parked outside. She saw a policeman talking to the man at her door who was not visible from her vantage point at the window. 'Help!' she cried to the policeman, startling him. He ran over to the window, followed by his colleague.

'The burglar's in here.' Joan stepped away from the window and pointed to the door of her bedroom.

The two policemen climbed into Joan's house through the window within seconds and stormed the hallway – but there was no young man there. They went to every room and even looked in the cubby hole under the stairs as well as searching the loft, but nothing untoward was found. Then there was another heavy knocking at the door, and one of the policemen answered. It was one of their superiors, a smartly-dressed detective, and he said: 'We've got him, love. He was hiding in a garden in the next street.'

Joan went outside with the policemen, even though the detective advised her to stay inside and make herself a hot sweet cup of tea. About a hundred yards down the avenue, was a car that had crashed into a lamp post and an ambulance was parked close by, lights flashing. The body of the young man Joan had seen crouching in her hallway was sprawled out on the smoking bonnet, and blood from his ears and nose was trickling in little rivulets across the car's crumpled bodywork. His head had caved in on impact with the granite cladding of the lamp post. His eyes were wide open and he was obviously dead. Joan was speechless. She saw the other young man – the one who had fled from the stolen car after it had crashed, and he was blonde and so small as to be childlike. He bore no resemblance to the dead youth, who had been thrown through the windscreen to have his head smashed against the lamp post.

The officers took Joan back to her home and she began to tell them that she had seen the youth with the appalling head injuries in her hallway. She had thought he had been a burglar, but now she realised he had been some sort of ghost.

And sure enough, after Joan returned to her house, she went into the kitchen, and was just filling the kettle and lighting the gas ring, with trembling hands, when she heard a voice in the hallway, 'My head! My head, oh God!' said the agonised voice.

Joan was so terrified, she took the backdoor keys from a drawer in the kitchen and walked through the night to the house of a former neighbour named Rose on North Sudley Road in Aigburth. Rose went back with Joan to her home later in the day – and she too heard the plaintive agonised voice in the hallway, but by now the voice seemed faint and indistinct. With time, the voice faded away completely, and Joan Chapell-Simons was visited for a few hours each day by her niece, who kept the widow company and was a great comfort to her.

There are many cases such as this where it would seem a person has died so quickly, they have become confused and tried to run away from the scene of their own death. I researched the case and discovered that the dead teenager's aunt had lived at the Rose Lane end of Brodie Avenue, so perhaps in post-death shock, the lad's spirit had been searching for her.

Faculty X

One blustery November day, in the late 1960s, the driver of a Hackney cab named Jimmy Quirth spotted a fare outside Blacklers. She seemed such a lovely old woman, and she was struggling with five bags and three boxes as she approached Jimmy's cab, shouting something he couldn't quite make out. Jimmy left his vehicle and unburdened the lady of her load, then opened the door to his taxi, which was always kept in an immaculate condition. He was about to return to his driver's seat, but before he could get into the cab, he heard a car horn behind him somewhere, and before he could turn, he found himself being rammed through the open door of his vehicle, which came off its hinges with the gargantuan impact.

Jimmy felt no pain, but lay there on his side in a dreamlike state of shock, watching the people from the bus stop near Yates's Wine Lodge running towards him. The world had tilted 90 degrees, and suddenly he felt weak and paralysed, as if his mind had become detached from his physical body, and the street seemed to fall away below him. He was now was floating high over Great Charlotte

Street. He passed Dickie Lewis, the sentinel statue of Lewis's, and somehow sensed he was about to see what all the dead see – the face of their Maker. Jimmy had led a fairly decent life and had no fears of his Judgement Day, but he woke up on his side with soft pillows under his head, and he focused on the green wall of a hospital ward before him and realised he had survived some kind of terrible accident. He'd been hit by a car, the surgeon told him, and had sustained minor brain injuries.

Jimmy's brother, Frankie, came to see him bringing with him the usual grapes, liquorice allsorts and Lucozade. Jimmy specifically asked for the framed photograph of his beloved late wife Lorna, and on his next visit Frankie duly brought in the monochrome memento and placed it on Jimmy's locker. That evening, in the hospital ward, at around ten o'clock, Jimmy lay there, head bandaged, gazing at Lorna's photograph. He could still hear the soft sweet timbre of her voice, five years after that dreadful disease had stolen her. Time had not healed the loss, and Jimmy never looked for another woman, for Lorna had been a one-off. In his inner eye he replayed some of the loveliest memories of the days he had spent with Lorna.

These reminiscences were interrupted by a most curious incident. Jimmy thought he saw Lorna's photograph brighten for a moment, and then his late wife's head actually moved in the frame. Was he dreaming? No, he was wide awake. Lorna blinked. She smiled and tilted her head quizzically as she gazed at the shocked cabby. 'Jesus,' Jimmy gasped. He turned to the man in the next bed – and saw that he too was wide awake and already spellbound by the animated picture. 'Can you see this, mate?' Jimmy asked the patient, who nodded without taking his eyes off the living picture. The man seemed scared, and he sat up wide-eyed in his bed as if he was witnessing the advent of a ghost. 'Oh, Lorna, is that you?' Jimmy asked, leaning towards the impossible image.

'Nurse! Nurse!' screeched the man in the next bed, then ducked under the covers.

Lorna's image became as still as a statue again. A nurse hurried into the room, and after hearing the patient's odd claim she reassured him he'd been dreaming. The patient swore and insisted that he had seen the picture of the woman moving, and he became so agitated they had to move him to the ward next door.

The moving picture had been no dream; it seemed that the brain injury had left Jimmy with an unearthly talent; he could bring photographs to life for a short while. Word of this strange new ability spread through the ward, and patients and their visitors crowded round the cabby's bed thrusting old photographs at him, and he would pass his hand over the pictures and sometimes they would move. Long dead loved ones would unfreeze from monochromatic Limbos and walk and gesticulate again as they had in life. A picture of a baby who had died aged three was seen to cry, and a WWI sepia soldier long ago killed in the Somme peered suspiciously from the dog-eared print at his beholders.

The chief administrator of the hospital – a lanky but stern-looking man with a military bearing about him – came down to see who was causing the ridiculous mania that was sweeping through the staffroom and the wards, and he found Jimmy Quirth sitting up with seven people sitting on his bed, and two of them were nurses! They were all engrossed by the miracle-worker as he passed his right hand backwards and forwards across a huge framed wedding photograph which seemed to date from Edwardian times. The newly weds – the grandmother and grandfather of the man who had brought the picture to Jimmy – smiled and looked at one another before the reanimated bridegroom leaned towards his new wife and kissed her in a rather self conscious manner. All seven people present gasped and giggled at the mysterious power of the animator, but then the hospital administrator coughed, and Jimmy, distracted by his presence, looked away, startled, and the Edwardian couple froze in their dead world of a print freckled with brown fungal spots and white crease-marks.

'Ah, do it again!' the couple's grandson pleaded, but the administrator told everyone to leave the ward. This was a hospital, not a place of cheap entertainment.

Only the nurses left, but the others stayed put. One woman held a photograph of a brother who had died when he was just seven, and she wanted to see him move again and interact, resurrected for a precious few moments in two dimensions. 'I want him to make this one move, and then I'll go, love,' the woman told the senior hospital official.

'No, come on, enough of these party tricks!' The administrator waved the sentimental seekers of lost time away, but they stood their ground, even when he raised his voice. Jimmy asked the hospital bigwig what the problem was; he wanted to know exactly what harm was being done.

The administrator accused Jimmy of being some charlatan, and the cabbie asked how anyone could produce the phenomenon he was producing by any sleight of hand.

'Hypnosis, perhaps, but please stop this nonsense,' the tall administrator now bent over him and looked at the moving picture of the woman's long dead brother. His jaw dropped. Another group of people bearing photographs, and some with whole family albums, arrived in the ward, and the administrator summoned several nurses and told them to keep the unofficial visitors at bay.

A few days after this, Jimmy was discharged from hospital, and when he got home, he discovered, to his horror, that his uncanny talent was failing. He concentrated for the last time on Lorna's photograph, and the face smiled, and with tears in his eyes, Jimmy raised the picture to his face and kissed the glass. His living lips kissed the colourless lips behind the glass, and he murmured, 'I will always love you, darling Lorna.'

And then this Faculty X vanished as mysteriously as it had first appeared. Years later, on a summer's afternoon, Frankie called at his brother's home, and could get no answer. He had a bad feeling about this, because Jimmy had suffered a heart attack only a month before, and so Frankie decided to kick in the back door of Jimmy's house. On the sofa in the living room, Frankie found his brother dead. He was staring at Lorna's photograph, and the life – the very spark of animation we all carry – had long fled from the cabbie's eyes, and now he was as still as the image of Lorna in her frame.

Moving images in otherwise static photographs and images that seem to come to life have been referred to before in my books, and I have touched upon a case where a Victorian photograph was haunted by an eerie figure which moved about within the motionless backdrop of a Bold Street captured in the 1890s, and I have also documented the case of a woman recovering from flu who saw a suicide re-enacted in an Atkinson Grimshaw painting of Whitby Harbour – which was indeed the scene of the very suicide witnessed by the Liverpool housewife. There is a statue in a certain well-known church on Merseyside which is said to move if you stare at it for a while, and even a priest told me (off the record) that he had seen the face of the statue smile. A cleaner at this church first noticed the weird phenomenon when she saw the head of the statue tilt and look down at her one morning.

Most scientists and psychologists would cite such cases as hallucinations. If you stare at a full moon for a while, it often seems to wobble because of an effect known as autokinesis. This effect occurs when a person observes a relatively small point or disk of light against a dark or black background. Although the disk or point of light is stationary, it will often wobble or appear to move because of errors made by the human brain between extraocular muscle control of the eye and the resultant misperception. Without a frame of reference, the brain cannot always estimate the size and position of an object – like a star or the moon – in a sky with no nearby object to compare the observed object with. Some UFOs are nothing more than bright planets and stars coupled with autokinesis, and even pilots flying at night have to be wary of the effect, especially military pilots aligning their planes to refuel in flight.

But there are some instances of moving images within photographs that cannot be put down to illusion. Footage was shown many years ago of the inmates of the infamous German-occupied Lódz ghetto in Poland circa 1943, which showed a curious scene which has never been explained. What appears to be two SS officers are looking at a corner of a room where a number of Jewish men and women are being detained, and they seem to be looking on in fascination at a small globe of light. When this light passes a framed photograph on the wall of the room, the figures within it begin to move. The light then fades and vanishes, and the figures in the photo revert to their previous static states.

I have always believed there is more to photographs than meets the eye, and the aforementioned incidents seem to vindicate my hunches.

MR MEDUSA

Between November 1887 and January 1888, a remarkable and eerie number of incidents were investigated by the police in Liverpool regarding an individual I have nicknamed Mr Medusa, because it was said that the evil gaze of this unidentified man's eyes could kill a victim or send him or her into a state of catalepsy and coma. So many of these cases investigated by the Liverpool Detective Office (which was located at 111 Dale Street at the time of these crimes) have been lost or destroyed down the years because stockpiles of aged files deemed of no interest were either misplaced or burnt or binned, to allocate space for modern files. I have, through my own research, managed to partially recover some of these intriguing cases, such as the Lizzie Peers and Madge Kirby murders of Edwardian times, but there are so many other crimes of interest from the Victorian era that still lie waiting to be rediscovered by the diligent and systematic researcher.

But back to Mr Medusa. One freezing evening at 8.40pm in the early November of 1887, as Bold Street was being peppered with a light fall of snow, a child's screams shattered the serene cold night air and sent a night watchman and a policeman running towards the source of the distress – Roscoe Place, a short blind alley that still exists at the top of Bold Street. That alleyway is fairly gloomy today, but in 1887 it would have been virtually pitch black at night. Police Constable Robert Longrigg (B172) and Charles Smith, a night watchman who had been at his brazier on Seel Street overseeing road works, came upon the heart-rending sight of a little boy, a shoeless street urchin, lying on his back, foaming at the mouth in the middle of a fit. His name was John Miller, and he was just eight.

The neglected child, who had wandered out of his hovel of a home off Pomona Street, was taken to the Royal Infirmary, where he regained consciousness after an hour. He told a doctor that he had been set upon by a man with 'horrible eyes' and as the child mentioned these eyes he began to sob and tremble. The doctor had heard an almost identical description from a girl of 16 who had been hit by a cart as she ran away from a man in a long black cape on Wolstenholme Square five days ago. The girl, Mary Williams, had been leaving the mill where she worked on Seel Street when the man, who was of below average height, had accosted her and tried to persuade her to retreat into the darkness of an entry with him with the promise of a crown. When Mary tried to run off, the man flew at her and seized her by the throat in with an iron grip of his leather glove. His top hat fell off during the assault, and even though there was a couple passing by on the other side of the badly lit street, the attacker kissed Mary then gazed into her eyes. The teenaged mill worker then saw the assailant's eyes expand into great black holes, out of which demonic eyes of pure evil appeared, their pupils glowing like hot coals. Mary felt faint and tried to look away but the satanic stranger's free hand ripped off her bonnet, gripped the bun on her head, and held her head still so she was forced to look into his eyes which spoke of Hell.

Sensing that her very soul was about to be drawn into those mesmerising pits, Mary managed to somehow let out a strangled scream and began to kick at the unearthly man, but it felt as if her shoes were kicking at a tree stump. The couple across the narrow street stopped and looked over at the caped monster. Then two burly men from the flour mill appeared on the scene to see why the girl was screaming, and Mr Medusa threw her down to the ground, picked up his top hat, and bolted off up Parr Street at an incredible speed, his cape flying upwards behind him. As he vanished round a corner, the heavens opened and there was a heavy fall of stinging hail.

That night, the doctor and PC Longrigg were interviewed by Detective William Allison, who took charge of the unusual case, and the scene of the attack was visited. Still visible in the fine layer of frozen snow were the shoeprints of PC Longrigg, the watchman, and the tiny prints made by the bare feet of Johnny Miller – but Detective Allison and two police officers saw something else by the combined light of their three bull's eye lanterns. A trail of very peculiar prints, made by abnormally elongated boot soles, were plainly evident in the layer of snow and ice on Roscoe Place, and these must have belonged to Mr Medusa, as Detective Allison had not noticed any oversized feet when he had interviewed the policeman and the night watchman. The freakish prints measured 17 inches in length, and their width, at the thickest point, was four inches, but tapered towards two inches at the toe-end. A policeman present quipped that he had he had only seen shoes that long on the feet of a circus clown. But even more bizarre physical facts about the uncanny attacker would later come to light.

In early December, a woman answered the door at her home on Beech Street, Fairfield (near the Kensington district of Liverpool) at 9pm one night, only to be greeted by the shadowy figure of a man about five feet four who wore a topper and an opera cloak. 'Hello,' he said to the woman, who was a housekeeper for a prominent businessman. Sensing the late caller was unhinged, she quickly closed the door in his face. The stranger knocked on the door again, and then he pushed open the letter box and looked in at the housekeeper, and saw the man's eyes 'light up' and glow with a reddish luminance. The housekeeper bolted the door and then ran screaming into the back parlour, where two servants responded to her cries. A butler left the house armed with a poker and saw no one outside, but he did notice the same abnormally long footprints in the snow on the pavement.

On the following night, just before twelve, the prowler called at the home of well-known wealthy tradesman, Arthur Russell, on Rufford Road, just a stone's throw from the house on Beech Street. On this occasion, the parlour maid stood at the front door with a candle, and was wise enough not to admit the caller. She asked who was calling at such a late hour and received a name in reply. This name was relayed via the servants to Mr Russell, and seemed to strike a chord with him, for he quickly instructed the butler to admit him, but when the door was opened, there was no one there. The butler went out to look up and down Rufford Road, but all was silent, and he could see nothing but falling flakes of snow. He then heard a scream from the hallway, and when he dashed inside he almost collided with a caped man in black, of medium height. The parlourmaid said Jane Burns, the young cook's assistant, who was just 15, had been attacked by a 'devil' with glowing red eyes. The fiend had sneaked into the house as the butler had gone in search of him outside, and he had even visited Mr Russell, who had been putting on his dressing-gown as he prepared to go down to greet the caller – who he had thought was an old business partner with whom he had lost touch. Mr Russell had found the face of the unknown caller to be so grotesque and terrifying, he had suffered a paroxysm and had collapsed from shock. Despite prompt treatment from a doctor, the wealthy tradesman never recovered from the disturbing encounter, and on the following morning his body was found lying on the floor of his bathroom. He had died from a suspected heart attack.

That same morning, Detective Allison and another detective named Bell interviewed Jane Burns, the cook's young assistant, and, still shaking and tearful at learning of the death of her employer, she described how, around midnight, she had seen a man roughly her own height (five feet three inches) enter the kitchen as she was preparing Brown Windsor soup for Mr Russell's supper. The cook, Mrs Jones, had not been present at the time. The man had worn a top hat, and a long black cape, but Jane particularly remembered his black moustache and very dark thick eyebrows which made him look foreign.

The stranger smiled at Jane, and then seized her by the shoulder with each of his gloved hands whilst his eyes bored into her. She saw the eyes change, followed by the rest of the face, and felt so scared at the sight of the metamorphosis she fainted. When she came to the butler was kneeling beside her with a glass of brandy. Detectives Allison and Bell examined the snowy ground outside the house on Rufford Road and soon picked up the traces of the attacker's extraordinarily long soles again. They were able to trace the tracks for almost a hundred yards in a straight line beneath the shelter of the trees until they became indistinct and then entirely obliterated at the end of the street, where new snow had fallen.

In January 1888, Detective Allison came home late one night to find his wife crying hysterically. She told him *he* had paid a visit – meaning Mr Medusa – the prowler with the face of a devil. The detective did not believe his wife for some reason and a row ensued. How on earth could the sinister attacker have found out that the detective on his trail lived at Number 8, Chalmers Street in the district of Edge Hill? This was the question Mr Allison posed, and his wife was at a loss to answer, but she said she would swear on the Holy Bible that the fiend had somehow gained access to the bedroom where she had been sleeping. At first Mrs Allison thought it was her husband standing at her bedside, but when she rubbed her eyes and squinted at the silhouette, she saw it was a man in a top hat, a hat her husband would not normally wear, and of course, she also noticed the small stature of the stranger. Then as she recoiled in horror at the realisation that an intruder was in her room, she saw two points of red light flare up where the stranger's eyes should have been, and only then did she realise that she was being visited by the very monster her husband had been trying to apprehend for weeks, and she began to yell and scream. She crawled out of bed, fell to the floor, and as the menacing silhouette walked across the bed towards her, she got to her unsteady feet and pulled the curtains open wide. She then lifted the window and screamed as if her life depended on it.

By the time she dared turn round, the bedroom was empty, though she thought she heard a door close downstairs, but she ran out of the house and stayed with a neighbour for a while until her nerves settled. The neighbour, a Mr Casey, had sat with Mrs Allison in her kitchen for over an hour after checking there was no intruder at large in the house. The deetctives rebuked his wife saying she should have called for a policeman immediately, but she said she had felt that would have brought ridicule upon her husband, with him being the very detective charged with the investigation into the baffling attacks.

Unsure what to believe, Detective William Allison slept very uneasily for a number of nights with his service revolver tucked under his pillow.

In the meantime, Mr Medusa was seen in the Wavertree area for while, where he perpetrated a number of attacks on young women after dark in several alleyways off Smithdown Road, and in April, he was seen prowling close to the Toxteth Workhouse, where the Sefton General Hospital would later be built and where the Asda supermarket now stands on Smithdown Road.

On Wednesday 25 April, 1888, he was seen running from the lodge of the Workhouse one evening, and when police later investigated, they were told that an inmate of the Workhouse – a 48-year-old attractive woman named Jane Porter, who had been employed as a servant at the lodge, had been found dead in her bed with a look of pure horror upon her contorted face. A woman named Margaret Mashiter shared the bedroom at the lodge with the dead woman, and told how she had found her companion dead in her bed at around 1.30am. The eyes were bulging and looking towards the door, which was ajar. Margaret shook her friend repeatedly, thinking she was drunk or had perhaps suffered a fit, but the body fell sideways and the face fell face down into the pillow.

On the stairs of the lodge, Margaret found a strange item – a finely-made black leather glove – for six fingers! A reporter from the *Liverpool Mercury* got wind of this strange story but someone in high authority seems to have hampered any reporting on the attacks of the mysterious assailant (and possible murderer). Detective Bell was convinced that hypnosis was being used by the attacker, and he mentioned the purported use of mesmerism in the notorious Gouffé affair – a brutal murder where the killer was said to have been hypnotised into slaying a victim. Detective Allison thought otherwise. He believed that some twisted maniac with a penchant for pranks had taken his tomfoolery too far. The oversized boots, the six-fingered glove, and the glowing eyes – possibly some gimmick achieved by the use of the mineral fluoro-spar, such as Blue John, being painted on to spectacles. But whether he harboured a belief that Medusa was something supernatural will never be known.

That April, in 1888, elderly man Arthur McKeown called at the detectives' office on Dale Street and asked to see Mr Allison. Allison came out to see the old man, who, in a Scottish burr, told him that the perpetrator of the attacks was not human at all, but some sort of bogeyman. Detective Allison probably listened to the old Scotsman with some bemusement as McKeown claimed that some 70 years ago, when he was a boy living up in Knockendoch, in Dumfries, he first heard about the man whose eyes could kill. Some thought he was a witch, and others believed he was the devil, but Mr McKeown's father had stated that he was a creature from an invisible world which runs alongside our own – the very same world the fairies and other supernatural folk inhabit. Every so many years, decades perhaps, the creature would take on human form and go in search of souls and the emotional energy humans give off when they are petrified. The thing was nourished by this energy, McKeown stated, matter of factly, at which point Detective Allison made an excuse to leave the old Scotsman. But as he turned and walked away, McKeown shouted out that he was sure the assailant was the same as the one at large up in Scotland because of the unusually long feet, and he added that the entity would also be found to have 12 fingers and as many toes, and this stopped William Allison in his tracks, because the six-fingered glove found at the scene of the Workhouse attack had never being publicised. All the same, policemen deal in facts, not fancy, and Detective Allison continued to believe that there was a rational explanation behind the assaults – but the case was never solved, and there were no further attacks by Mr Medusa after the end of April 1888.

A new monster was soon grabbing the headlines that year, and his name and dark deeds totally eclipsed the career of Liverpool's mysterious assailant. He was, of course, Jack the Ripper.

Humpty was Pushed

In 2009 a fairly-well known local comedian was doing his stand up at a popular comedy venue in Liverpool. To this performer, who we shall call Sean (not his real name), no subject was taboo, and he delighted in making the audience squirm with his comedic, but often dark, close-to-the-knuckle observations about society and the absurdities of human behaviour.

Sean was excelling himself that night, but at one point in the routine, he noticed a rather large bald-headed man who was sitting with a beautiful foreign-looking woman at a table quite close to the performance area. The bald man was not laughing, but had the most miserable expression on his face as he watched the comedian.

From the low stage Sean shouted, 'Crack a smile, Humpty!' and everybody laughed – except the man to whom the remark had been made and his female companion; a sparse wintry grin broke out on her face but the eyes did not smile. Sean then went on to do his routine about the way the lives of the younger generation revolve around mobile phones, and he had the audience in stitches with his surreal gags.

And then he came down from the stage, wiped the beads of sweat from his face with a towel, and was about to leave the club, when the bald overweight man came hurrying over to him. The comedian thought he was going to have a go at him for being called Humpty, but instead the man smiled, and thrust his hand out to Sean. The two men shook hands briefly, and the bald guy said, 'Sean, I'm a big fan of yours. Your timing is brilliant, and you really stand out from the other comedians because you have that eye-to-eye contact with the audience. They call it rapport ...'

'Ah, thanks, mate, that's lovely,' Sean said, relieved there would be no trouble.

'That eye-to-eye thing,' the bald man went on, 'makes it feel like you're talking to each and every one of us.'

Sean started to think this fan was a little bit 'out there' and when he looked into the stranger's clear blue eyes, he sensed there was something missing – something dangerously unstable about him.

'You don't look well, Sean, are you okay?' the bald man asked with apparent concern.

Sean was about to contradict him and say he felt fine but felt ill all of a sudden. Nausea made his head swim.

The man touched Sean's chest and said, 'You haven't got chest pains have you? Sean? Are you okay, man?'

Sean flinched from needle-sharp pains in the centre of his chest.

'This man's having a heart attack,' the bald man said to the foreign-looking woman he'd been sitting with, and she got up from the table and the couple eased Sean down into the chair the overweight fan had sat in throughout the performance.

'I'm okay,' Sean was saying, but the fan was telling him not to panic, and that he'd call an ambulance. He asked Sean if he had pains going down his left arm. Sean shook his head, but still felt terrible.

'Do you have erm, sharp, shooting pains going down your left arm to your wrist? Sharp pains, not dull ones?' the fan asked.

And suddenly, as Sean listened to the over-attentive fan babbling on, he lost consciousness.

He awoke in blackness, and could not feel anything. He tried to speak, but his tongue just lay there in his mouth and did not even twitch, as much as he willed it to move.

Suddenly, there was a loud grating noise, accompanied by a vague sensation of movement. A bright neon-lit ceiling swam into view, and Sean had the dim sensation of warm hands pulling him by the forearms and legs. He was being dragged out of a wall. It didn't make sense at first, and then he realised he had been taken out of a clinical white drawer. He saw the chin and nostrils of a man in white garments, and he was being viewed from below. Sean got it now. He had died. He had died in the club and had just been taken out of the body drawer at the local morgue, but where was this guy taking him? He was being pushed along on some trolley, and he could see the long rectangles of neon light scrolling past as he was pushed along some corridor.

Sean passed through several doorways with doors that swung open with a bang as the trolley headed towards its ominous destination. 'Am I still alive or is this what death is like?' Sean asked himself in a mind swimming with confusion. And then the trolley reached the autopsy room, where the coroner waited.

'Sean (and the surname was given here), date of birth ...' the coroner checked the data sheet. 'Heart attack at a nightclub, third of April 2009. Let's have a look.'

The mortuary worker transferred Sean's body on to the slab. Sean thought the coroner would see that his pupils were shrinking in the harsh halogen lights trained upon the slab, but for some reason he had a radio on somewhere, and he was humming along to the music it was playing, and seemed quite oblivious to any such little tell-tale signs of life.

Sean summoned all his willpower to try and move his eyes, but it was useless.

The coroner, with a mask covering the lower half of his face, came into view, and pulled back the eyelids of Sean's right eye and shone a penlight at the pupils. Surely the light would make the pupils contract?

The penlight was switched off, and then a hand clad in a rubber glove could be seen, and it was holding a scalpel. The coroner began to sing along with a Frank Sinatra song that was playing on the radio: 'You make me feel so young ...' as he inserted the blade at the base of Sean's neck, just a few inches below his Adam's apple. A faint sensation of pain, of icy steel sharpness, reached Sean's mind, as if he was under some anaesthetic that was wearing off perhaps. He could feel the blade being drawn down towards the direction of his chest, and he could feel the blood that was still liquid even after the heart had long given up. He could feel the stale clotting blood dripping syrupy from the rolling incision. The scalpel passed down the centre of his chest and down towards his navel. It cut the through the belly button and halted just above the pubic area. What a nightmare! What a time to get philosophical! Sean thought about his wife and young son at home. Had they been informed of his death? How were they taking it?

'Hey, Sean!' cried a voice somewhere.

Sean felt a glimmer of hope. Had someone arrived to tell the coroner to halt the post mortem because Sean had been admitted to the mortuary by mistake?

It was the coroner addressing the mortuary worker, who, by a dark coincidence, was also called Sean. The comedian's heart sank – if it was still beating, that is.

'Sean, pass that dish, I need to put the heart in it,' said the coroner, and then he put his hands into the gaping slit – into the chest cavity – and pulled the body open with a revolting squelching sound. Then he slowly rummaged around in the ribcage and took out the heart after slicing through the vena cava, the arch of the aorta, and the left pulmonary artery, as well as bunch of stringy veins and tissues. The coroner lifted the heart up out of the chest, and Sean felt sick, for now he knew he was definitely dead. His consciousness was still persisting, and that was a mystery. He knew now that there was no hope of ever being resuscitated. The next stop was the grave – or was it to be cremation inside a coffin on a conveyor belt in some furnace? Would Sean's wife have him burned to a crisp or would he be placed in the ground to swell and rot? Sean had heard the stories about the pelvis being the only part of the body that was left intact after thousands of degrees of prolonged intense heat. He had heard how the staff at crematoria were said to grind the pelvis that remained into powder to mix into the ashes …

And what if his consciousness still persisted as he lay in a cold eternally black grave? Forever blind and deaf, where no sights and sounds would ever reach him till the end of time.

There was a loud buzz. The coroner was using some sort of rotary saw now.

'You taking the brain out?' asked the mortuary worker in a raised voice so he could be heard above the din.

'Yes!' the coroner shouted back.

'Oh no, oh no!' Sean said in his mind as he saw the circular blade coming towards his eyes. The blade made contact just above the eyebrows and made the eyeballs vibrate, so that everything became a blur, and as the blade went in, all of the stagnant jellied blood dripped over Sean's eyes ...

Sean found himself back at the club, seated at the table with the fat bald man and the exotic-looking woman. The man was holding Sean's left wrist – feeling for a pulse. The singer on the stage was belting out the Sinatra song Sean had heard moments before. 'You make me feel so young!'

'I was dead,' Sean muttered, and the man nodded and smiled.

'Yes, you were, dear,' said the woman, with a seductive East European accent.

'It was all a dream?' Sean looked around, feeling light headed. His mouth was bone dry.

'I did it,' said the corpulent man.

'Did what?' Sean was so confused could hardly hear them because of the Sinatra tribute act.

'Never mind,' the fat man replied, and let go of Sean's wrist. 'Don't ever call me Humpty again.'

The woman's dark eyes twinkled as she smiled at Sean. 'Humpty was pushed,' she said, 'and he could have killed you tonight. No one could have proved a thing.'

At this the couple left the table and Sean headed for the toilets to be sick. He could still see his excised heart and feel the sickening whirring of the rotary saw as it penetrated his skin, skull and brain.

On the following day, Sean asked everyone in his acquaintance if they knew anything about the odd couple he had been sitting with last night. Did anyone know that fat bald man? One of the bouncers claimed the man was a stage hypnotist who had gone down in the world because of ill health, and only then did it all start to make sense. The hypnotist had put Sean into a trance when he had directed him to look into his eyes and then, by talking about eye to eye contact had put it into the comedian's mind that he was not feeling well, that he had chest pains and was experiencing a heart attack.

It transpired that, during the trance, an old drunken friend had called out to Sean, and the comedian had heard the voice calling for him as he was experiencing the realistic sensation of being on a mortuary slab, but the hypnotist had told the friend Sean wasn't well and he had then told Sean that the mortuary worker was named Sean. Had the trance proceeded any longer, it's likely that Sean would have run the risk of dying from shock; a form of death which can take place when certain susceptible people have nightmares about falling from tall buildings or cliff tops. Most wake up before they hit the ground, but others have woken up and suffered heart attacks, and so it is likely that some have even died in their sleep from the trauma induced by the nightmare.

THE VAMPIRES OF HARTINGTON ROAD

The following story came to light during research for my book *Vampires of Great Britain*, but the account came a bit too late to be included in the work.

In the mid-1960s, Norman a Liverpool man in his mid-forties, was knocked down and killed in a hit and run accident in Manchester. Norman had one living relative – an aunt who lived on Cantsfield Street, off Smithdown Road in Wavertree; all of Norman's other relations, together with all his immediate family, had died in various tragedies and it was said that Norman's family had been cursed, but no one knew who was supposed to have cursed them or why they were damned. What is known, and this was well-documented, is that when Norman's coffin was sent back to Liverpool to be buried in Toxteth Park Cemetery (on Smithdown Road), shrieks were heard by the driver of the mortuary van transporting the coffin.

The driver kept what he had heard to himself at first, probably fearing that he would be accused of hearing things, or maybe he was, like most people, scared of the unknown and the supernatural, and did not want to know how, or why, a coffined corpse was screaming, but then as the coffin was being taken to a chapel of repose, the pallbearers – all four of them – felt it shake violently and heard what sounded like a faint scream and a gurgling sound come from within.

A pathologist was contacted and when the coffin was opened he found that the corpse of the hit and run incident was in a very peculiar state. The eyes were wide open, and the complexion was a ruddy colour, quite unlike the usual grey pallor of death, and the lips too were very red. After death, the skin usually turns green, then purple, and finally black, but on some rare occasions it remains stable and fresh for some inexplicable reason, so the pathologist bore this odd fact in mind as he examined the corpse.

Within three hours of death, calcium seeps into the muscle fibres, causing the limbs to stiffen, and so begins the condition of stiffness known as rigor mortis. And yet the limbs of Norman's corpse were very pliant and flexible, and the blood in the cadaver's veins showed no signs of decomposition, or settling. As the coroner examined the mouth, the body emitted a long fart. Such flatulence from the dead is common, resulting from of a build-up of gas as bacteria literally eat the intestines from within and produce methane and other gases as a by-product of fermentation. But the coroner thought he also traced a faint grin on Norman's face.

A mortician of some experience was on hand to assist the coroner, and he could see that his professional colleague was quite unnerved by the facial expression of the corpse, which was now definitely grinning; there was no mistaking it. The muscles of the face often relax in death and cause what is known as the 'Dead Man's Smile'. The coroner seemed very eager now to conclude his examination and the corpse was soon replaced in its coffin for a straightforward funeral service attended only by the priest and the pallbearers.

But that was far from the end of the matter. The burial took place in a communal grave on the western side of Toxteth Park Cemetery (which lies adjacent to Hartington Road) during a thick October fog, and of course, the communal grave had no headstone or any marker to show the place where nine other people were lying dead in a stack in the cold clay.

Three days later, on Halloween, another blanket of fog of a celadon hue crept over Liverpool in the late afternoon, bringing with it all sorts of perils to the rush-hour traffic. By lighting-up time

Toxteth Park Cemetery was a black opaque swirling mass, and some people passing this city of the dead on Smithdown Road and also Hartington Road, reported hearing strange shrieks coming from the western side of the fog-enshrouded cemetery. At around 12.40pm that night, there was a faint knocking at the door of a house on Hartington Road, which brought Audrey, a 21-year-old music student, from her first-floor lodgings down to her draughty hallway. Audrey thought the late-caller would be her friend, who often visited her at unearthly hours, but when she opened the door, she got a nasty shock.

A tall man with a weird blue caste to his skin stood there. Not only was she alarmed by the caller's deep eye sockets with their tiny glimmering red points of light where pupils should have been, but his purple jacket and dark trousers were filthy with muck, as if he had been rolling about in mud and his receding hair too was encrusted with dirt and stood up in ugly little tufts

The tall stranger suddenly grinned as Audrey asked timidly, 'Can I help you?' But she didn't wait for a reply as she had just spotted something even more alarming about the man with the blue-tinged skin – a pair of yellowed fangs, such as are only seen in horror films or in the mouths of lions and tigers in the zoo. Slamming the door in his face she ran upstairs, two at a time, and locked herself in her room, where she went to her window and peeped through a gap in the curtains. The fanged man was now flitting away from the house and quickly vanished into the misty shadows. Audrey desperately wanted to leave her room and go across to her friend Vaughan's flat, who like, Audrey, was also a music student, but Audrey could hear him playing his cello, and didn't want to disturb his practice as she knew he had an important exam coming up. However, as it was getting rather late to be playing an instrument, Vaughan soon stopped playing, and left his room to go down to the communal kitchen to make some cheese on toast.

Audrey decided to go down to the kitchen to tell Vaughan about the weird caller, and when she did, Vaughan thought she was joking at first with it being Halloween (then widely known as Duck-Apple

Night) because this night of all nights was associated with ghosts, vampires and so on, but Audrey's serious eyes soon conveyed the validity of her account.

Nevertheless, Vaughan thought some Halloween prankster had been at work, but Audrey just knew no hoaxer was responsible. She recalled the freakish man's burning red eyes and shuddered. Vaughan asked Audrey if she'd like some cheese and toast but she declined, and instead she sat at the little kitchen table that was spread with pink gingham cloth and enjoyed a coffee and a cigarette. Vaughan put the bread under the gas flame grille and then he went to the window, cupped his hand against the pane to block out the dreary 60 watt bulb's light. He gazed up over the backyard wall at the moon – high in the sky and a little past its full phase – barely showing through the upper, but thinner reaches of the fog.

The kitchen door flew open, so suddenly that Audrey nearly choked on her coffee, and Vaughan's head twisted to face the sudden movement.

A shapeless cloud of brown smoke or vapour billowed into the room, then began to condense, until they coalesced into the distinctive form of a tall man. Audrey screamed and ran towards Vaughan and hid behind him shaking with terror. The air crackled with what sounded like static electricity, and Vaughan and Audrey backed towards the kitchen door leading to the rear yard. But that door was locked, and neither student knew where the key was. The murky faceless figure stood there in the centre of the room with smoke swirling around it. Vaughan picked up a carving knife that had been left in the sink with the usual pile of unwashed dishes, and hurled it with some force, squarely at the menacing apparition. The knife passed straight through the gaseous figure, but as it did so there was a flash of light and a dull thud from the 'ghost'. The figure suddenly began to fade, leaving no evidence of its visit, other than a thin mist hanging in the tense air of the kitchen.

Audrey and Vaughan looked aghast at the spot where the manifestation had existed just seconds ago, then fled the kitchen, taking care to avoid the space where the smoky being had stood.

Vaughan took Audrey up to her room where they both sat, for a long while utterly lost for words.

'Do you think it was the man who called earlier?' Audrey eventually asked, biting her nails. And when Vaughan didn't reply straight away she added: 'The man with the fangs.'

'I think I should tell my brother about this,' Vaughan suddenly announced, breaking out of his silent contemplation.

That night, the cello player slept in an old armchair in Audrey's room, keeping watch over her in case the ghostly entity returned, but there were no further visitations from the thing that night. On the following morning, at around ten o'clock, vestiges of the fog were still lingering when Vaughan and Audrey walked to the telephone box on Smithdown Road, where Vaughan dialled his brother John and recounted the strange events of the previous night. John said he would call at his flat at 2pm that afternoon, and he was true to his word, arriving about five minutes before the arranged time. Audrey was very surprised when she saw that John was a young Catholic priest. Vaughan offered his brother a sandwich, but he declined and asked him to try and describe what they had witnessed, both individually and together in the kitchen. After listening to their accounts, Father John spent a long time, deep in thought.

'I thought it was someone mucking about at first, when Audrey told me about the fangs,' said Vaughan, 'with it being Duck Apple Night and that.'

'No, it's no one mucking about, Vaughan,' said Father John gravely.

The two sat there, tense with expectation, as they waited for some enlightenment from John.

'Well?' Vaughan said with a lopsided grin born of nerves. 'What the hell is it then?'

The priest looked at his hands, and his long dark eyelashes flickered for a moment. 'It sounds ... and I know this sounds ridiculous ... but it sounds ... like a vampire,' he replied, and as he said this, Vaughan's alarm clock in the room stopped ticking and a silence descended on the room.

Three pairs of eyes shot over to the clock.

'You alright, Audrey?' Father John asked, smiling weakly.

Audrey smirked and blushed, saying, 'A vampire? Really? You mean like Dracula?'

'Nah, he's pulling our legs,' Vaughan said with a hollow little laugh and patted his brother's forearm, but the priest gently but resolutely shook his head.

'I'm not pulling anyone's legs,' he said, coldly now. 'These things were accepted by the early Church, and they date back to Ancient India, Babylonia and Ancient Greece.'

'What ... vampires?' Vaughan tried to laugh it off, to dismiss the strange talk, seeing the fear welling in Audrey's eyes.

'I'm being serious ... vampires,' Father John replied, 'Some are turned into vampires and some have always been vampires, and no one is safe ... even priests.'

Then John told them about a strange incident, which made Vaughan feel very uneasy because he vaguely remembered being told about it. It had happened when he was around twelve, ten years ago. As he rubbed his hand and looked into the two incandescent bars of the electric fire, Father John mentioned a certain Catholic church in Liverpool, and a story he had heard about this place of worship from an elderly priest.

John said that in the 1930s, two cleaners arrived at the church at around half past four one February morning to mop the aisles and polish the altar rails. As one of the cleaners, a woman in her thirties named Violet, was mopping the transept, she happened to glance over at the pulpit, where she thought she saw a figure with some white about it duck down out of sight with amazing reflexes. Violet thought it was a trick of the light at that time in the morning, because just enough of the lamps had been switched on in the church for the cleaners to go about their work. However, when the aisle was being mopped about 20 minutes later, Violet passed the pulpit, and once again she thought she could detect some movement high up inside the ornate raised platform. She continued to mop, and then suddenly, she literally felt the hairs on the back of her neck stand on end. Ever since the cleaner was a child she had possessed the uncanny talent of feeling eyes burning into the back of her head if anyone was watching her from behind. She stopped her mopping and turned her head very slowly to see a strange and scary sight up in the pulpit.

A priest she had known when she was a girl, was leaning over the rail of the pulpit. He was the very priest who had been present when Violet made her first Holy Communion. He had died many years before, for Violet, like most of the late priest's congregation, had attended his funeral. The ghostly priest's posture was rather strange. He was peeping over the pulpit rail with his arms bent, and his eyes were black and glistening. The apparition made a hissing sound, and Violet threw down her mop and ran down the aisle in a terrible state, slipping on the wet floor at one point. Then she heard the screams of the other cleaner, and when she looked across the benches, she saw the old priest swooping down on her colleague like some gigantic bird of prey. The both managed to escape from the church, and vowed never to clean that church again.

When the church authorities heard of the strange incident, they tried to hush it up, and even paid the cleaners to say nothing of their terrifying experiences. But then strange rumours began to circulate in the parish. It was claimed that the elderly priest, whose ghost had haunted the two cleaners, had told someone shortly before his death that certain shocking secrets about his life would come to light and tarnish his reputation, but the old man would not be drawn into further conversation regarding these secrets. All sorts of gossip circulated concerning these alleged secrets, and some scandal-mongering parishioners even claimed the old priest had dabbled in Satanism, holding Black Masses at the church in the dead of night.

The elderly priest who had related this story to Father John had allegedly discovered the real truth though, and claimed that the priest who had worried about his reputation becoming besmirched after death had been nothing less than a fully fledged vampire, but it was never explained just how he had become one. Two experts in vampirology and demonology were dispatched from Rome to rid the church of the entity. Exorcisms and other arcane rituals were carried out in the locked church, but a curious night watchman, who managed to use a ladder to peek into the church through the stained-glass windows, described a spindly-looking figure in a long black cassock climbing the walls of the nave like a spider and flying across the altar as the exorcists confronted it – until, the thing was seized by the men, and brutally staked through the heart!

'Enough!' Audrey cried out, and Father John and Vaughan jumped with fright at the sudden exclamation. 'Stop it, please!' the girl cried. 'I've heard enough.'

'I'm sorry, I'm sorry,' the young priest apologised and reached out to comfort Audrey but she ran out of the room and went to her own room, followed by Vaughan and his brother.

'See what you've done now?' Vaughan berated his brother as the two men tried to get through the doorway of Audrey's room at the same time. The priest apologised profusely and promised the young student he would protect her from the thing that had materialised in the kitchen the previous night. The priest had read a lot about vampires and knew there was a pattern to their attacks. Often, a girl of a certain age, usually a virgin, was targeted by the vampire for grooming. The virgin's blood, or any woman for that matter (especially those who had recently given birth), was thought to be particularly desirable to the blood and life-energy suckers, and this was probably why Audrey had been targeted, although Father John didn't dare tell the anxious girl this for obvious reasons. The vampire had probably been doing a little reconnaissance before the attack, trying to establish whether Audrey was alone, or whether she had someone to protect her. Father John felt that the entity was likely to attack that night, and so he sat alone in Audrey's room during the hours of darkness, with nothing but a Holy Bible, a crucifix, and a bottle of holy water for protection. Audrey, meanwhile, was sitting with Vaughan in his room playing cards as she periodically took nervous glances at the alarm clock.

At one in the morning, the vampire made its dramatic entrance, this time not using a gaseous form, but a carnate, solid form. It must have lifted the cast-iron manhole cover from the pavement outside (which would require considerable strength) to gain access to the coal cellar. It then forced the coal cellar door and emerged in the darkness of the hallway on the ground floor. Father John heard the slow measured footfalls on the stairs, and knowing that the two residents of the flats on the ground floor were old people who would now be tucked up in bed, went out on to the landing with a large crucifix in one hand and his personal black leather-bound copy of the Bible clutched in the other hand.

The first thing he saw were the red points of light – the eyes of the vampire – as it came to a halt at the top of the stairs. The thing uttered a string of vile swear-words as well as making several blasphemous references, but the priest reached out with the hand that held the Bible and used his index finger to switch on the landing light. As the dim 60-watt bulb came on, the vampire could be seen in its grubby soil-stained attire. It reeked of something sweet and sickly but indefinable, and it shielded its blood-red eyes from the meagre electric light. 'In the name of Jesus, in the name of Yahwah, I command thee to return to your grave!' Father John boldly addressed the undead being.

'You sanctimonious self-abusing hypocrite!' replied the vampire in a raspy voice, and spat at the priest, ejecting some ghastly yellow and green foaming fluid with great force. The glob hit the Bible which the priest was using as a shield.

The vampire-laying prayer was recited: 'Rest eternal grant unto him, O Lord, and let perpetual light shine upon him!'

'We'll have her!' the vampire spat out the words and made rude gestures at the priest, and walked slowly along the landing with its skeletal hand with its yellowed fingernails shielding its face from the sight of the cross and the Holy Book.

The priest was trembling, and sweat was forming on his brow. He wondered what the thing meant when it said 'we'll' have her; was there more than one vampire? He steadied himself with thoughts of how Jesus would act in this situation and continued to recite the prayer: 'Kyrie eleison. Christe eleison. Kyrie eleison. Our Father. And lead us not into temptation, but deliver us from evil. From the Gate of Hell, O Lord, deliver his soul. May he rest in peace ...'

The vampire jumped up into the air and punched the light bulb, shattering it into a myriad of orange sparks and glass shards. The landing was now in semi darkness, with only the feeble light shining out from Audrey's room, where the priest had been lying in wait.

Audrey's screams pierced the air in Vaughan's room. The door of that room opened and Vaughan's head appeared round it. 'There's something in here!' he shouted, and then he noticed the shadowy figure standing near him on the landing, and swore in shock.

'Get back in there!' Father John shouted to his brother, then lunged forward and pushed the crucifix almost into the face of the revenant. It howled, and there was something animalistic about the way its jaws opened and the way the mouth enlarged to reveal the elongated teeth and fangs. It fled back down the stairs, with the priest hot on its tail. Upon reaching the bottom step he could hear more screams coming from Audrey upstairs and the sounds of objects being thrown about. John switched on the light, then went after the vampire. When he reached the coal cellar, he saw it fly upwards through the disk of orange light – the manhole illuminated by a sodium lamp. The creature slammed the manhole cover down on to the hole with a clang and could be heard running off.

Father John left the cellar, and ran back up the stairs to tackle the thing in his brother's room, but he collided with Audrey and Vaughan as they rushed blindly down the stairs to escape whatever was pursuing them. Audrey screamed and pushed the priest aside as she ran down the stairs, and Vaughan followed her closely, urging his brother to get out of the house.

'For Heaven's sake don't go out there!' cried the priest, 'That thing is out there!'

He then turned to see a swirling mass at the top of the stairs, like a thousand black flies all assembled in the form of a human figure, and it moved forwards with a very peculiar gait. This was probably the thing which had materialised in the kitchen on Halloween. Vaughan and Audrey had surmised it was just another form of the vampire that had called at the house, but now it was obvious that there were two entities at large.

Instinctively, the priest threw the Bible at the insubstantial figure as it came down the stairs, and as the book passed through it, it vanished after dissipating into tiny particles which quickly faded away.

Audrey and Vaughan witnessed the dematerialisation of the ghost, and felt a little safer when the priest joined them in the hallway.

'What now?' Vaughan asked his brother.

'We should sit tight until dawn if we can,' John suggested, and he went into the parlour as Audrey and Vaughan embraced one another in the hallway. He was gone for some time, so Vaughan shouted into the dark parlour: 'You alright in there?'

John came out of the parlour and what little colour had been in his face had now drained away. 'Let's go to the kitchen,' he said in a low voice.

'Why?' Vaughan asked, his suspicion mounting, 'Why? What's up?'

One of the doors to the ground floor flats opened and a door-chain rattled. A pair of bloodshot eyes peered out from the gap and Audrey yelped with fright. An old man complained about all the noise, he was trying to get some sleep, then with a shaking fist he closed the door and put the security chain back on.

Upon reaching the kitchen, John switched on the lights and went to the window. He pulled a blind down. 'There's more than one,' he said, despondently.

'I gathered that,' Vaughan told him, 'the thing upstairs was one as well, wasn't it? That's the one I saw in the kitchen ...'

'I counted about ten of them out there,' the priest said, and Audrey's eyes widened. Father John would be haunted by the look of pure fear in those young eyes for many years to come.

'Ten?' said Vaughan.

Father John nodded, then asked his brother if there was a hammer and some nails knocking about. In a daze, Vaughan opened the cupboard under the sink and grabbed the black rubber handle of a large claw hammer protruding from a box. He pulled it out and searched for a while for some nails, but all he could find was a box of old rusty tacks. 'Better than nothing, I suppose,' the priest remarked upon opening the little cardboard box. 'Stay here,' he said firmly, then left the kitchen with the hammer, tacks and crucifix. The priest made sure the bolt was firmly fastened on the front door, and then he tried to tack the coal cellar door shut but the tacks just weren't long enough, so he went back to the kitchen and found a length of old washing line, which he used to secure the cellar door by tying the door's handle to the stair rail. But there were still so many other ways the vampires could enter the house, and if things got too hairy the priest warned they'd all have to make a run for it – even though the thick fog had returned and was now covering the whole of the North West.

The three young people sat in the kitchen with a gas ring continually burning for warmth. Audrey sat holding hands with Vaughan at the table, as they listened to the sound of bony fingers scrabbling at the window, and a host of other unnatural noises. Shadows flitted across the window blind, and then, at around half-past two that morning, the trio heard a sound they could not ignore in the hallway. Audrey began to cry, imagining the vampires had gained access to the building. John and Vaughan cautiously crept into into the hallway. Vaughan carrying the hammer, and his brother clutched the crucifix. Now it was possible to tell that the sound was coming from the front door. The vestibule door was open – which led to the small space behind the front door – and there the brothers saw a long reddish-purple arm, almost bone, covered with suppurating lesions and scabs. It was so narrow it had been able to slip through the letterbox and now the skeletal hand was trying to undo the bolt.

Vaughan suddenly lashed out with the hammer. He smashed the upper arm with such force, it broke the humerus, and the sound of the brittle bone breaking made the priest nauseous. The thing behind the door shrieked in agony and tried to pull its arm away. The arm below the break dangled, lifeless, attached solely by the skin, and as the brothers backed away from the rattling door, the arm was withdrawn to agonising howls of pain. The letterbox then snapped open, and a pair of eyes that can only be described as demonic, stared out at the two men with intense hatred.

'I command you to leave here in the name of Jesus Christ our saviour!' Father John intoned.

The letterbox flap banged down, but then lifted a few seconds later, and this time a grotesque purple tongue wormed through it in some warped act of mockery. The vestibule door was closed and the two men were startled by Audrey, who frightened to be left on her own, had left the lonely kitchen to see what was going on.

All three retreated to the kitchen, where they sat tense and mentally drained from their ordeal. When dawn eventually came filtering through the fog, and they could hear the reassuring sound of the milkman clinking the bottles on their doorstep, Audrey announced that she was getting out and had no intention of ever coming back to that house on Hartington Road.

Over the past few weeks, Vaughan had begun to realise how much he liked Audrey, in fact until the events of the last few days had interrupted the quiet transition from friendship to romance, he had thought of little else. He decided that he too could never stomach another night in that place, so he asked Audrey if she would consider moving in with him if he could find a decent place to live. She agreed to give it a try, and within two years she and Vaughan were married.

Father John left the priesthood 20 years later, after becoming disillusioned with the attitude of the Church towards the paranormal, which he studied until his death in 2003.

I mentioned this case on the radio in 2002 and had quite a few calls about strange goings-on at the house on Hartington Road, as well as at a few other addresses on that road which lies next to Toxteth Park Cemetery. All of the accounts lead me to suspect that vampiric entities were at large in the area in the 1960s, and I think some of these beings – including the infamous 'Manilu' a vampire I have written about in many of my books – are still active. In particular, I believe one of these vampires is the etheric form of Norman, the man I mentioned at the start of this section, who was interred in the western side of Toxteth Park Cemetery in the mid-1960s.

Of all the supernatural beings in the pantheon of mythology, the vampire seems the most far-fetched, and yet across the centuries –

millennia even – everyday people have reported encounters with these sinister beings which defy death itself and siphon off the lifeblood and vitality of the living. At the time of writing, I and several other investigators of the paranormal are looking into an alleged case of vampirism in Hoylake, where a mother and teenaged daughter are being visited nightly by a shadowy entity which materialises in their room. This being takes on the form of a monk with a pointed hood, and often when the thing appears to the mother or daughter, always at around three in the morning. It leans over them in their beds and paralyses them before sucking at their necks. After about five minutes, the entity fades away, and sometimes contracts to a gaseous dark nebula, which drifts off through the windows, leaving the victim feeling drained and ill.

What makes this case particularly interesting is that I recently unearthed a report from 1971, involving two teenaged girls, living within a stone's throw of Hoylake railway station. They were subjected to nightly attacks by a shadowy form which paralysed them in their beds and sucked at their necks.

Around 1978, there was a similar case reported at a house on Woolton's Quarry Street, where a woman was subjected to an almost weekly assault by a shadowy man who would float down on to her bed, paralyse her, then begin sucking at her neck and breasts. Paul, an investigator of the supernatural who has passed on many interesting findings of this nature to me over the years, looked into the case, and used an elderly medium who had been personally tested by himself. The woman claimed that the vampire visiting her had originally been a man who had been buried in Allerton Cemetery in the early 1970s, and through some biological process, had not been clinically dead at the time of burial. He had awakened in the stifling blackness of his coffin and through sheer willpower, had somehow projected what occultists would term the astral body, out of the grave. However, as the body's energy began to fade after a length of time, it would gravitate back to the grave, and so the buried man would go out and search for a new source of energy to replenish his 'etheric' body, so it could stay out of the rotting shell of its decaying physical body. It would seem that all bodies, even before they decay in the grave, become separated from their astral counterpart, but in this case, the man who had been prematurely buried in Allerton Cemetery had somehow convinced himself he would end up six feet under unless he kept 'topping up' the energy of his astral body, hence the regular attacks on various women over the years.

In the end, the medium said she had contacted the restless anxiety-ridden spirit and had explained why it had nothing to worry about, but the advice was ignored, and so maybe then, the vampiric entity is still making its nocturnal attacks.

THE ROMANCE OF INANIMATE OBJECTS

Juliet went into her bedroom one mellow sunny September afternoon and decided she would exorcise the ghosts of her wardrobe. Every dress, every top, every pair of shoes and every coat had a tale to tell, ranging from the early 1970s to just a few years ago. Her friend Jane had beheld the vast time capsule of Juliet's wardrobe and had told her she was a sentimental fool. 'Sell those old dresses to the vintage shops, make some money and free up some space,' Jane had advised, and when Juliet had admitted that the boots and handbags and jam-packed multi-coloured decades of haute couture and tackiness were like old friends, Jane raised cynical eyebrows, pursed her lips and folded her arms. She finally persuaded Juliet to bin-bag most of the wardrobe, and every time Juliet would say, 'Oh, I've got to keep this striped top – the Chelsea look; remember?' Jane would shake her head and open the bin bag wider.

And so, that September afternoon in 2003, Juliet and Jane took the clothes to three main vintage clothes stores in Liverpool, and what could not be sold went to the charity shops. Juliet took one last pensive look back from the doorway of the Oxfam shop as a young female shop assistant held up a fuchsia Mary Quant dress against her friend and smirked. Juliet got home with the little money she had made from the sale of her memories, and it felt like 30 pieces of silver in her purse. She opened her wardrobe door and listened to the echo of nothingness in the room. She actually cried.

A few days later she was shopping on Bold Street, when she noticed a girl of about 20 walking ahead of her, and she was wearing a Rajah suit in silk with a very familiar floral design of orange and gold. Straight away Juliet knew it was her old suit – the one she had bought in the Lucinda Byre boutique, on this very street, Bold Street, in September 1973, exactly 30 years ago. And that long-haired girl looked exactly like a young Juliet, at least from the back.

Juliet quickened her pace. She had to see the girl's face. The sun broke through as she went in manic pursuit. What a curious case of history repeating itself! Now the 'young Juliet' was hurrying towards a long-haired teenager in a brown suede jacket and grass-green flared trousers – the double of Chris Gardener! In that very Rajah suit, in September 1973, Juliet and boyfriend Chris had met here at this exact same spot and gone to the Red Pearl Restaurant next door to Mappin & Webb on Ranelagh Street.

A grey-haired debonair man of about 50 approached Juliet's double and said something to her, and the young couple eyed him with half smiles. And then they walked away. The grey-haired man was none other than Chris Gardener – a man Juliet hadn't seen in 20 years. He saw Juliet and with a look of astonishment, pointed to the teenaged couple in the distance and Juliet nodded rapidly by way of acknowledgement. Juliet and Chris embraced, and went to a café, where Juliet said, 'Did she look anything like me?' And Chris gave a curious reply. 'They *were* us ... We somehow met our younger selves today,' he said, deadly serious, and squeezed his old flame's hand. The flame of their love was rekindled in that moment and they married a year later, and Juliet eventually bought most of her old clothes back.

In 2005 a reader named Mark was going through a bad patch in his life. He had broken up with Lisa, his girlfriend of four years after he had found her flirting on his computer with a man via MSN Messenger and a webcam one afternoon when he had come home from work earlier than normal. It soon transpired that Lisa had been seeing the man, Jack, for almost six months. A row ensued and Mark stormed out of their flat and never went back.

Now he was facing a Christmas on his own, something he had not experienced for quite a few years. He had texted a few of his mates and received no reply, so one morning in late November 2005, Mark decided to go to a café he hadn't been to since around 1999. He chose this café in Everton for one reason only – Barbara – the beautiful redhead who had served him his full English breakfast all those years ago. Unfortunately, Mark learned from one of the staff that Barbara no longer worked there; she had left just over 18 months back. This was a real pity, because he wished he had shown more interest in her all those years ago, instead of chasing Lisa.

Mark thought about two things as he sat reminiscing in the window seat of the Everton café: his mother, who had sadly passed away from cancer three years back, had always said Barbara was a lovely girl and had tried to persuade him to take her out. She had even gone so far as to say that Barbara was Mark's soul mate. Mark's mum used to claim to able to see auras around people and had told Mark his aura was the exact same shade as Barbara's but he had just laughed it off. The second thing he recalled was the morning he had got talking to Barbara and had been on the verge of asking her out. He had gone as far as asking for her number and she had actually given it to him. Mark smiled as he recalled writing down the landline number on the back of a ten pound note.

A song came on the radio in the café which had, he recalled, been Barbara's favourite: *Pure Shores* by the British/Canadian girl group All Saints. Could this be a sign? Mark smiled wanly as he drank his coffee. His mother would certainly have interpreted the song as a sign that he should go and look for Barbara. Where on earth would he start though? Mark vaguely recalled she lived in the Cabbage Hall area of Liverpool.

Just then a man tapped Mark on the shoulder and said, 'Hey, lad, have you got two fives for this?' and he presented Mark with a dog-eared ten pound note.

'Yeah, I think I have,' Mark said, and he delved into his wallet as the man explained how he owed his mate sitting at the table five quid but didn't have the change. Mark handed the man two crisp new fivers he had taken from a cash machine earlier, and the man smiled and nodded and handed him the ten pound note.

And Mark couldn't believe his eyes, for there, on the back of the tenner, was Barbara's phone number, and next to it. There was no mistaking it, because next to it, all those years ago, Mark had doodled a little heart. The chances of this happening were, of course, astronomical. Mark took out his mobile, looked at the number on the banknote, then put the phone back in his pocket. He still had lingering doubts. Say Barbara had moved and someone else answered that landline? He'd feel an idiot asking for Barbara. And say she was married now? A lot can happen in six years. She might have kids now, and she'd probably think he was a weirdo calling her out of the blue after so many years.

Mark left the café and went to visit his mother's grave. At the graveside, he looked about, made sure no one else was within earshot, then whispered to the black granite headstone: 'Ma, you probably know all about the phone number on the tenner, and how I feel about Barbara. I never listened to you all those years ago, but now I wish I could hear your advice. Mam, please tell me what I should do.'

And after a few moments deep in thought, Mark sadly walked away from the grave and distinctly heard a woman's voice shout: 'Go to her!'

Mark stopped and turned around, thinking someone was behind him, but saw no one. It was eerie yet very thought provoking. Mark left the cemetery and went to the nearest pub in order to build up some Dutch courage to make that call. After a few pints and a short, he finally plucked up the courage to dial the number. The phone rang eight times, and then a man's voice answered.

'Er, hello there. Can you tell me if Barbara's there? It's Mark,' and of course, Mark gave his surname.

'I'm her husband, David,' the man replied coldly, knocking the wind out of Mark's sails. 'Do you want to leave a message with me?

She's out you see.'

'Nah, no, it's not important, er ...' and Mark hung up, utterly deflated. As he put his mobile back in his pocket, it started to ring, and Mark looked at the number on its display screen; it was the number he had just dialled – Barbara's number. He rejected the call. Then about a minute later the phone bleeped as a text message came in, from Barbara's husband, it read: 'Who are you? Are you seeing Barbara?'

Mark cursed himself for being so stupid, and switched the mobile off before heading for a bus stop. On the bus home, he thought about Barbara again, and put himself through unnecessary misery by wondering what would have happened if he had dated her all those years back. When Mark got home he could hardly eat a thing. He was always snacking, always in and out of the fridge, making himself sandwiches, but his father noticed the way he just sat there on the end of the sofa, and asked him what was up.

'Nothing's up, I'm okay,' Mark told him, but he couldn't fool an old perceptive soul like his dad.

'Not hungry?' his father queried, and he heaved himself up out the armchair and switched off the television. 'Not like you, Mark.'

'Nah, I've just been to a café, I'm okay,' Mark replied, and picked up the *Daily Mirror*.

'Oh,' was all his dad said, sitting back down. He looked at the little tattoo with the faded blue-green name of his late wife on the skin of his forearm.

'Dad, do you believe in ghosts and all that ... like Mum?' Mark suddenly asked.

'I'm not sure,' he said. 'I've never seen a ghost, but I know people who've said they have. Why?'

'I went to me mum's grave today, and I asked her to give me advice, about a girl like.'

'Go on,' said Mark's father, intrigued.

'I told me Mum I should have taken her advice about that girl ... Barbara ... d'you remember her?' Mark asked, sheepishly.

'The red-headed girl, yeah,' his father replied. 'You never shut up about her at the time.'

'Well I asked me mam what I should do, and this is no word of a lie, Dad, but after, when I was walking away from the grave, I heard a voice, and it sounded exactly like me mam's voice, and she shouted: "Go to her!" and I looked back, expecting me ma to be standing there, it was that clear.'

'Your mum really liked Barbara didn't she?' his dad recalled.

'Yeah. What d'you think? Was it her voice?'

His father inhaled deeply, raised his eyebrows and shrugged. 'It's one of those things isn't it? You know, the supernatural, whatever you call it, is always like this. It's always fifty-fifty either way; there's never anything concrete about it. It could have been someone you couldn't see in the cemetery.'

'There was no one around for at least two hundred yards, and even that was a little old woman, Dad, and anyway the voice didn't come from her direction.'

Mark's father felt a bit uneasy and he pulled a cigarette out its packet and searched for his lighter. The cigarette wagged between his lips as he spoke. 'Yeah, but sound travels funny in those places. Must be the acoustics, with sounds bouncing off the headstones.'

The television came on by itself, and there was All Saints singing *Pure Shores* on the MTV channel; a channel that Mark's father never watched.

Mark's jaw dropped – Barbara's favourite song, the one that had come on the radio at the Everton café.

'What's up with the telly? Why did that just come on by itself?' Mark's father asked, searching for the remote. 'That's with you talking about spooks,' he joked.

Mark left the living room and went upstairs to try and get his head round this eerie situation. He played a few CDs and then noticed a curious coincidence. On the floor was a CD by Abba, and beneath it was a CD of Edwin Starr's songs. The Abba CD covered the Edwin Starr CD in such a way as to only show the last three letters of his name. Mark realised that the letters ABBA ARR spelt BARBARA when they were jumbled up. Barbara was taking over his mind, he needed to get a grip, so he dismissed the anagram as pure coincidence.

His head in a whirl of painful emotions, Mark went to the corner shop to buy a magazine and a newspaper, and as he set foot in this shop he heard a voice cry out his name. He turned and saw it was an old friend named Mal who he hadn't seen in years. The two men got talking and Mal said he was working in a local garage nowadays. The two friends then continued their chat outside the shop, and in the course of the conversation, Mark mentioned Barbara and asked Mal if he remembered her from the café in Everton.

He nodded and said to Mark: 'Oh yeah, the red head, yeah she er she ...'

'She got married, I know,' Mark butted in.

'No mate ... she died.'

The world seemed to stop at that point. An ice-cream motor had been playing its jingle-jangle melody and a group of kids had been screaming and shouting and playing war games, but all these sounds faded as Mal mentioned Barbara being dead.

'Hang on, she can't be dead, I talked to her husband today,' Mark said with confusion in his eyes. 'I found her old number you see, and I decided to give her a bell, like, and her fellah answered. He said she was out. I'm sure he would have said if she was dead.'

'No, she definitely died,' Mal said gravely, and he could see Mark was gutted at the news. 'Yeah, the redheaded girl,' said Mal remembering her and nodding slightly. 'Not sure if it was cancer or an accident. Hey listen, mate, give me your number and we'll keep in touch. We can meet up in town one night.'

'Yeah, that'd be great, said Mark in a daze.

Mark gave Mal his mobile number and drifted off back to his home. He went upstairs and in the quiet of his room, he whispered: 'Mam, if she's dead, why did you say go to her? I know it was you, but I just don't understand.'

About a week later, Mark was sent to town on an errand for his father, who wanted him to pick up a few tins of gloss paint and some brushes from Rapid Hardware on Renshaw Street. Mark had just got off the bus when he saw her. There was no mistaking her: that beautiful head of red hair, and that face which didn't show the slightest trace of ageing since he had last laid eyes upon it. It was Barbara alright, and when she saw him, she slowed, and shot him a look of slight amazement. She smiled shyly, and Mark's heart quickened. No girl had ever made him experience the feelings he was having now. He could hardly get his words out. He hugged her and she hugged him back, and then he apologised for not ringing her all those years ago, and then for ringing her home the previous week. He asked what her husband had said about his cold calling.

Barbara was puzzled by his last question, for she had no husband, nor was she living with anyone. Then she realised what had happened. Danny, the man who had moved into her old flat after she had moved out, had had a weird crush on her, and had stalked her for a while, even sending letters to the local radio station, asking DJ's to play dedications for his fiancée Barbara. He told everyone he was engaged and then married to her. He had psychological issues, but was probably harmless.

Mark and Barbara went to a café on Bold Street and talked and talked, and at one point their hands slid across the table and met. Mark showed Barbara the ragged ten pound note bearing her old number, jotted down next to a heart by him all those years ago, and she thought it was all so romantic. 'I believe …' Mark began to say, and he couldn't believe he was coming out with this, because he was not the romantic type, but he blushed and said it anyway, 'Well, I know … I'm sure … that we were destined to fall in love.'

That evening, Mal texted Mark. The message read: 'That redheaded girl deffo died. Her name wasn't Barbara either, it was Bev and she had lookeemia (however u spell it) …' With enormous relief, Mark then realised that Mal had been thinking about another red-headed girl. He never told Barbara about his mother's voice from beyond the grave, as it would probably have spooked her.

Mark and Barbara each found the one they had been looking for, for so long. They later married and are still happily wed.

The Thing in the Bedknob

If you're looking for a weird story, you've come to the right chapter. The following odd account was told to me many years ago by a man named Gordon, who came to a booksigning at the now non-existent Borders bookstore in Cheshire Oaks. I have looked at the tale from all sides and considered all sorts of explanations: carbon monoxide build up in the boy's bedroom, which might have caused hallucinations: natural fluctuations in the zero point energy field, beings from beyond our dimension meddling with time and so on, but all the theorising throws little light on the strange phenomena and transcendental experiences of a 13-year-old boy all those years ago. See what you make of it all.

One bitterly cold November night in 1959, when the boy had just turned 13, he lay in an old double bed in a draughty room at his Auntie Mo's house on Catharine Street, in the city centre, almost facing the old Women's Hospital. His name was Jack, and his mother was in the maternity hospital on Oxford Street, where she was expected to have her third child within the next few days. Jack's father was a drunken lout and Mo had taken the boy into her care until her sister recovered from childbirth. Mo had said that Jock, as she called Jack, because she was Scottish, could stay as long as he wanted at her humble home. Mo had always wanted children but had never had any. This was a great pity, because Mo was a loving person with a great maternal instinct, and in the place of children, she had a clowder of cats that she doted on, who were always coming and going at the house, via the catflap in the back-kitchen door.

Well, Jack was put in the old bed and because Mo was rather careful with her money, she said he could only have the light on in his room for an hour, and then he was to go to bed, or he could light a candle and read by that. Jack had been in bed for about 40 minutes when Mo came up to his room with three of her cats. She turned off his light saying sleep was the best medicine, and that Jack should stop straining his eyes reading his comics and go straight to the Land of Nod.

'The land of what?' Jack asked.

'The Land of Nod, Jock,' Mo replied, 'it's in the Bible, in Genesis, to the east of Eden, aye. The land where you go when you nod off. Don't they teach you anything at your school?'

'Auntie Mo, before you go, can you tell me why you've got socks on the bedknobs?

She turned round and returned a rather odd nervous look at this question. 'That's not for you to wonder about, laddie, now get to sleep.'

'Nanight,' said Jack, in his usual lazy way of speaking.

'And a good night to ye as well.' Mo went out, gently encouraging the nosy felines.

'Nanight, cats!' said Jack. His little head gazed out from the covers. As soon as his auntie had gone, Jack got out of bed, lifted his pillows to locate the box of matches, and promptly lit the candle stub in the old brass candlestick. Now he had to find out why his barmy aunt had put thick woollen socks over each of the bedknobs. He started with the sock on the bottom right bedknob. He lifted it and looked at his face in the gleaming coppery-brass globe. He was just about to put the sock back on the bedknob when he saw something move within it. At first he thought it was the reflection of the candle's spluttering flame, but there were two lights moving in the globe. He stepped back from the eerie face which appeared in the mirror-like surface.

A spectrum of colours were now glinting off the bedknob, and the creepy face was now clear. It was ovoid, golden-skinned, with pointed ears, and a widow's peak reminiscent of Dracula which went down to the bridge of the nose, which was long, pointed and aquiline. The eyes were black, almond shaped and had pinpoints of yellowish white light where the pupils should have been. Jack was about to scream, but a little hand appeared in the bedknob and an index finger was pressed against the entity's mouth, as if it was gesturing for him to be quiet. Jack's fear of the little man's head was allayed slightly by this gesture, but he remained stock-still and very wary. A soft faint word-perfect voice came from the being's flickering mouth. 'Be very, very quiet or I shall go,' it said.

Jack gulped. 'Who are you?'

'Never mind who I am,' said the weird face, 'you look bored and I can take you places. Do you want to come with me?'

'No,' Jack replied firmly, 'I don't want to go with you. You look scary.'

'Suit yourself, byee!' the imp of the bedknob smiled and became smaller and smaller until there was only the reflection of Jack's face in the brass. Jack got back into bed as the cold started to bite, and rather stupidly he sat up, placed the candlestick on his lap, and cupped his hands around the flame in an effort to gather some warmth. As he did this he kept his eyes peeled on the uncovered bedknob, as he now had the unsettling feeling he was being watched.

And he was right.

The tiny golden faced being appeared in the bedknob again. 'I see!' he said in a shrill tone.

Jack jumped at the sudden reappearance. He thought about running out of the room to find his aunt and to this day, Jack does not know what made him stay put in the bed. Perhaps he was too cold to move.

'Come with me, Jack!' the sinister creature injecting some volume into its soft voice.

Jack went cold inside upon hearing the thing refer to him by name and it gave him a bad feeling.

The candle sputtered and went out, and as Jack was looking for the box of matches, he saw the bedknob glow like a light bulb, and its multi-coloured rays gave the orb a prismatic appearance.

Jack was mesmerised by the rainbow display of colour and his eyes felt heavy. He suddenly kicked his leg in the way some people do when they wake themselves up on the edge of sleep. After the jolt, Jack found himself in a very strange place. The buildings were mostly sleek and futuristic, but some of them were old in comparison, and he realised it resembled Liverpool's Catharine Street, but it wasn't the Catharine Street of 1959; it looked more like 2059 – like something out the pages of the *Eagle* comic. The cars were aerodynamic with crystal bodies from which a green light shone, and others hovered as they moved silently along a silvery road. Some cars were airborne and they flew in great arcs and figures of eight in the sky as they avoided one another. Jack didn't feel real; as if he wasn't really there.

He hurried down a side street near to what would be Caledonia Street in his version of reality. The paving stones beneath his bare feet felt rubbery and emanated a serene sky-blue radiance. Coming down the street of light was a gang of some sort, and as they got nearer, Jack could see they were a bunch of girls dressed in the strangest clothes he had ever seen. Some wore huge shoes with thick soles, similar to the ones the Teddy boys in 1959 sported, only these had much thicker soles and were shiny as vinyl. Some of the girls wore white tights with horizontal bands of garish colours, and two of them wore bizarre blue fur garments that covered the same area as a bikini in Jack's time, but what really stood out were their outlandish hairstyles. One had a gigantic beehive like something out of the days of Marie Antoinette's, and one girl had a huge spiky purple head of hair with lights twinkling in it.

As the girls came nearer, Jack heard them all using very coarse language, and he distinctly heard the girl with the huge beehive brag that she was going to do something crude to a boy, which really shook Jack and scared him a little. He hid behind a pink dome-shaped car as the gang passed by, and when they stopped on the corner, Jack could see most of the girls had strange tattoo-like patterns on their faces, and some even showed their bare breasts. They talked in a very queer language. He heard one of them say what sounded like 'frinight' when the other one asked her when she was going to some event, and Jack realised the slang was for Friday night. The gang talked rapidly and all at the same time, uttering weird phrases he could not comprehend. And then something terrifying took place ...

A young man with hair as long as a woman's (in the eyes of Jack) came on the scene with an extraordinary unicycle of some sort. It was like a scooter with a wheel absent, and as the man tried to drive past the gang of girls, one of then fired something that looked like a silver wire with something at the end of it resembling a ball. This ball curved around the young lad's neck and the wire was tugged violently. The male came flying off his unicycle and the girls all cheered and started kicking him and stamping on his head and body. As the attacked man screamed for mercy, Jack saw one girl crouch and stick out her fist, and from a ring on her finger came a green spray of some gas or fine liquid, and the victim screamed even louder as the spray hit his eyes.

Jack sneaked round the other side of the car and then ran off, putting as much distance between himself and the crazed female gang as possible, but at the other end of the street he saw yet another gang of girls, and this time every one of them was dressed in black. All of them had huge hairstyles, almost like the fur helmets of the guards at Buckingham Palace, and these girls carried whips, and what looked like medieval maces with spikes sticking out of them. Their faces were chalk white, and this gang of Gothic looking females wore black boots with spikes running down one side. Jack turned and ran off as he heard a whip cracking behind him and screeches of laughter. Almost in tears, he wanted to be home.

He felt a jolt in his body again, and found himself hanging out of the bed in his auntie's spare bedroom. He got to his feet and ran out of the room and along the landing to Aunt Mo's bedroom and barged in. She was snoring with her dentures in a glass on her bedside cabinet and on her bed were three of her older cats. They watched Jack as he shook his auntie awake, and she let out a shriek, and swore at him. Then she opened her eyes and saw it was only her nephew.

'What d'you think you're doing trying to give me a heart attack?' she said, and then, as Jack began to try and rattle off his account of the weird goings-on with the thing in the bedknob, Mo told him to look away for a moment, as he continued to give his garbled account. Mo screeched at Jack to shut up, and again told him to turn away for a few seconds. The baffled boy did as he was told, but took a sly glance over his shoulder and saw his auntie grab her false teeth from the glass and insert them into her mouth. 'Now, you were saying?'

Jack told her all about the golden-faced entity in the bedknob that he had uncovered, and before he could say any more, Mo said: 'After all that I told you, you went and took the socks off those bedknobs! They're not covered up for nothing you know! You're not sleeping in that room any more, laddie, it's the sofa for you from now on!'

And she meant it too. For the remainder of the time he spent there, Jack slept on the sofa in the living room, and was never allowed to go back into the spare bedroom. When he went back to his own house to see his mother and her new baby, a girl named Daisy, he told her about the face in the bedknob and of the bizarre futuristic street he had found himself in with the gangs of violent weirdly-dressed girls, but Jack's mum was a simple woman, and she merely smiled at his account of the strange goings-on, and ran her hand through his hair.

Jack then asked his father why Auntie Mo would put socks on her bedknobs and was told that Mo was known as a very eccentric woman. For years, Jack wondered if he had dreamt about the impish being in the bedknob or whether it had actually existed, and if it did, was it some entity that had somehow allowed him to travel into the future? It's a very unusual case which has haunted Jack for decades. He is in his sixties at the time of writing and still has nightmares about the golden-faced thing in the bedknob.